The Cure for Love

De-ann Black

First published 2011

This paperback edition published 2021

The Cure for Love

ISBN: 9798520837503

Also by De-ann Black (Romance, Action/Thrillers & Children's books). See her Amazon Author page or website for further details about her books, screenplays, illustrations, art and fabric designs.
www.De-annBlack.com

Romance:

The Sewing Shop
Heather Park
The Tea Shop by the Sea
The Bookshop by the Seaside
The Sewing Bee
The Quilting Bee
Snow Bells Wedding
Snow Bells Christmas
Summer Sewing Bee
The Chocolatier's Cottage
Christmas Cake Chateau
The Beemaster's Cottage
The Sewing Bee By The Sea
The Flower Hunter's Cottage

The Christmas Knitting Bee
The Sewing Bee & Afternoon Tea
The Vintage Sewing & Knitting Bee
Shed In The City
The Bakery By The Seaside
Champagne Chic Lemonade Money
The Christmas Chocolatier
The Christmas Tea Shop & Bakery
The Vintage Tea Dress Shop In Summer
Oops! I'm The Paparazzi
The Bitch-Proof Suit

Action/Thrillers:

Love Him Forever.
Someone Worse.
Electric Shadows.

The Strife Of Riley.
Shadows Of Murder.

Children's books:

Faeriefied.
Secondhand Spooks.
Poison-Wynd.

Wormhole Wynd.
Science Fashion.
School For Aliens.

Colouring books:

Summer Garden. Spring Garden. Autumn Garden. Sea Dream. Festive Christmas. Christmas Garden. Flower Bee. Wild Garden. Faerie Garden Spring. Flower Hunter. Stargazer Space. Bee Garden.

Embroidery books:

Floral Nature Embroidery Designs
Scottish Garden Embroidery Designs

Contents

Chapter One

In the heart of a London park

Art and Sebastian were Daisy's greatest passions. In the heart of a London park she was enjoying both — sitting on the grass painting watercolour flowers and daydreaming about Sebastian. It was the perfect blend of work and pleasure on a bright, sunny day. She worked as a freelance botanical artist, mainly for Franklin's publishing company, painting floral illustrations for books. That's where she'd met Sebastian. He worked in editorial. She'd been dating him for two years and he'd been hinting recently that he wanted to get married. If he asked her, she'd say . . .

While she considered the perfect response, a car drove up and parked illegally, ignoring the disapproving stares of people nearby. The driver got out of the car and hurried towards her. Sebastian was devilishly handsome, tall, with light brown hair, and had the appearance of a successful young businessman. At thirty, he was one year older than Daisy.

She was too busy with her watercolours and daydreaming about the engagement to notice him approach.

When he asked her to marry him she'd say . . .

'Daisy,' Sebastian said, causing her to make a wild brush mark across her painting.

'Hell's bells, Sebastian — what are you doing here?'

He bent down, swept her blonde hair back from her face and kissed her. Daisy was naturally pretty, with a slender but curvy figure, and soft, pale skin that Sebastian said he adored. According to his circle of acquaintances, she was completely not his type, and judging by his history of entanglements with tall, leggy brunettes they were probably right. Daisy admitted she didn't have a type. Three and a half boyfriends were the sum total of her relationships, in four different categories — loud, quiet, stupid and vain. Mr vain only counted as half because he'd dumped her while he was working abroad and it was weeks before she realised as he'd forgotten to tell her.

1

She went to kiss Sebastian, but he'd already focussed on her work, casting a critical eye over the ruined painting. 'Call it an abstract,' he said. 'A bad clash of colours there anyway.'

She frowned at her artwork.

'Never mind that,' he said. 'I had to see you before I left.'

'You're leaving?'

'I'm going to the publishers' convention in Italy. Franklin's tied up with the book packagers' deal, so I'm going instead. I'll be back in a month.'

'A month?'

'I wanted to see you before I caught the next flight.'

'How did you know where to find me?'

He pulled her close and looked into her clear green eyes. 'I always know where to find you.'

Before she could open her mouth to complain, sob or shout, he kissed her passionately, and then glanced at his wristwatch. 'I have to run. I'll miss you.'

For a moment he became quiet and looked at her lovingly. He touched her cheek and a flicker of guilt crossed his face.

'What's wrong?'

Sebastian smiled. 'Nothing.'

He kissed her again, long and hard, before making a dash for his car.

As he ran off he called back to her. 'Don't let Phillip near your artwork. I don't want him making any stupid alterations. And ignore any suggestions from editorial. Leave them to me. Oh, and keep an eye on Franklin for me. He listens to you.'

Daisy smiled and called after him. 'Anything else I can do for you?'

'Yes, love me forever,' he shouted.

The sky darkened and clouds shielded the sunlight as she watched him hurry away.

In the distance, Sebastian paused, spun around and looked at Daisy. She waved at him. He waved back, got into his car and drove off.

The breeze picked up speed, blowing her sketch paper away and spilling water on her other paintings, ruining them. The sky darkened further, threatening a storm, causing her to shiver. She collected her artwork and managed to streak her clothes with watercolour paint in the process.

It was raining. Daisy ran across the crowded London street towards Franklin's publishing company using an umbrella to cover her artwork portfolio. She'd been working like a demon all week to take her mind off Sebastian. He hadn't contacted her, which was usual. He hated anything interrupting business. There was something familiar in his actions that she was strangely comfortable with. It reminded her of when she was a child, how her parents would drop everything, including her at a friend's house, and fly off to exotic locations. They were an adventurous pair, which she admired, but she'd happily have settled for slightly boring but more available parents.

Leaving her wet umbrella at reception, Daisy made a beeline for Franklin's office. He was pleased to see her. Franklin was a tall, dashing figure in his fifties. He had a penchant for immaculate light grey suits and white shirts, worn with silk bow ties, his only indulgence in colour.

Daisy handed him a selection of floral artwork from her portfolio. 'Poppies, pansies and, I think you'll love this — wild flowers at night. I used a pair of night–sight binoculars so I could see to paint them in the dark. The things you can buy online are brilliant — and I got these earrings too — impulse buy.'

Franklin glanced at the artwork but seemed contemplative.

'Don't you like them?' she said.

Franklin looked at her. 'The earrings look great.'

'No, the artwork.'

'It's splendid.'

'Splendid? I know you well enough to decipher that splendid really means you like the artwork but your mind is on something else, something you don't want to ask me.'

'I need a favour, Daisy. You know the artist I commissioned to do a portrait of Celeste for her twenty–seventh birthday?'

'I heard he's recovering nicely.'

'He's agreed not to sue,' Franklin said. 'We're settling out of court.'

'Quite a temper your daughter's got.'

3

'She didn't like what he did with her nose. It was a bit skew–whiff.'

'What's the favour?' she said, biting back any remarks about Celeste's nose.

Franklin took a photograph of his beautiful but aloof daughter, Celeste, from his desk drawer.

'No, no, I can't paint Celeste. You know I don't paint people.'

'I'd like to give her the portrait when she gets back from Italy,' he said.

'Celeste's at the book convention?'

'Yes, so you'd have time to finish it.'

'I can't paint people,' she said.

'What about that bumblebee you did? His little face was so cute.'

'His stripes were the wrong way round.'

'Everyone thought you were being surreal.'

Daisy raised her eyes in mock surprise. 'Whatever gave them that idea?'

'And the cat, don't forget the cat,' Franklin reminded her.

'I'm not proud of that piece. We cheated.'

'We had a tight deadline to meet. Using the photocopier was sheer genius.'

She shook her head. 'It wasn't right.'

'The cat was fine. She's had kittens since.'

'No doubt.'

Franklin pushed the photograph across the desk towards her.

Daisy pushed it back. 'Bumblebees and cats aren't people. I can't paint faces.'

'The bee and the cat had faces — eyes, nose, mouth —'

'Fur and whiskers,' she said.

A man with a bushy moustache popped his head round the door of the office. He spoke directly to Franklin. 'The printers are shitting shoe horns.'

Franklin gave the man the thumbs–up. The man hurried off.

'I'll need to sort out the printers,' said Franklin. 'Will you please do the painting?'

Daisy looked at the photograph. 'Celeste hates me. She won't want the portrait if I painted it.'

'She doesn't hate you. She's just envious of your talent. I thought you could possibly scribble some obscure pseudonym on the

4

painting. Pretend it was created by a mysterious fellow from Europe. Celeste would love that.'

Daisy smiled. 'For a nice man you're terribly devious.'

'All men are. We just like to pretend that women are the ones of unfathomable depths.'

He handed her the photograph.

'No promises,' she said, putting it in her portfolio.

Daisy was working at night in her apartment in London, trying out various styles of sketches of Celeste, including unflattering cartoon drawings depicting her as a sly looking cat. Her artist's studio was set within a normally tidy lounge, though tonight numerous crumpled roughs of Celeste were scattered around.

Drawing faces wasn't her forte, and besides, her heart just wasn't in it. She missed Sebastian. And why of all people did Celeste have to be in Italy with him?

'I wish I was in Italy, and Celeste was in London,' she said, studying her latest sketch. 'And I wish I could get her blasted nose right.'

It took three weeks to get her nose right and finally finish the painting. With a huge sigh of relief, she zipped it safely inside her portfolio. It had been another long night. Never again would she paint a person, especially snooty Celeste.

Casting a weary glance out the window at the glittering lights of London, she got ready for bed. She was tired, irritable and felt lost without Sebastian. He hadn't answered any of the messages she'd sent to his hotel. Men! Men! Bloody men! But she still missed him terribly. Tomorrow she'd give Franklin the painting and then treat herself to lunch at her favourite restaurant. Sebastian would be home next week.

'Bloomin' typical,' she grumbled to herself. The morning was grey as charcoal, it was pouring rain and she'd had to park streets away from Franklin's building. Celeste's painting, inside her portfolio, got the full shelter of her umbrella. No way was she risking it getting soaked in this weather. Wet, bedraggled hair was a small price to pay to get it there undamaged.

Leaving the umbrella dripping at reception, she carried the bone dry portfolio through the open plan offices heading for Franklin's office. Everyone stared at her. Hadn't they ever seen someone with wet hair before?

At the far corner of the offices a small crowd had gathered. As she got nearer she saw they were drinking a champagne toast. Then the crowd parted to reveal Sebastian and Celeste standing together, back early from Italy. Celeste held up her glass in celebration.

Daisy's world flipped into slow motion. She could see the faces of the crowd staring at her as everything slowed right down. Celeste smiled and made sure Daisy saw the sparkling diamond ring on her engagement finger.

Sebastian stepped forward, and it took a few moments before Daisy could comprehend what he was saying.

'Don't be mad at me, Daisy. I hope you can find it in your heart to be happy for us.'

Franklin stood like a statue in the background.

The shock and anger hit Daisy hard, and the slow motion feeling was replaced with the urge to run away.

She dropped the portfolio, and it fell to the floor, opening at the finished painting of Celeste.

She left it lying there and turned to run away, but Sebastian grabbed hold of her arm.

'Let go of me, you bastard!'

She tried to break free, but there was a scuffle. Daisy threw a wild punch at Sebastian but he ducked down and Celeste got the full force of the punch right on her nose.

Amid the gasps and confusion, Daisy ran from the building into the crowded street. The noise of the city was overwhelming; everything was closing in on her.

Hearing Sebastian's voice calling after her, she ran off, disappearing into the crowd of umbrellas.

Daisy looked terrible — like a strangely attractive maniac running amok at night in her own house. She'd wept away the daylight hours, and was now busy trashing everything she had belonging to Sebastian.

The doorbell rang.

She opened the door to find her neighbour, Archie, a young man and an interfering idiot, standing there with an accusing glint in his eye.

Rage burned inside her. Tonight he'd come to the wrong bloody door.

'I heard noises,' he said. 'Is everything alright?'

'Everything's fine.'

'You seem rather . . .' he glanced at her hair and indicated that it was sticking up. 'Your hair is somewhat wild.'

Daisy sounded slightly aggressive. 'Wild?'

He rephrased tactfully. 'Windblown, yes, windblown rather than wild. The underground plays havoc with the hair gel.'

Her tone was fiery. 'This is the new me.'

Archie almost swallowed his Adam's apple. 'And very nice too.'

Daisy gave no further response except to glare at him.

He walked away, and she closed the door.

Fifteen minutes later she set off the fire alarm in her kitchen burning Sebastian's love letters in the toaster. By the time she managed to switch the alarm off (hit it with the handle of a floor brush), interfering Archie was back again.

'The fire alarm —'

'No fire, no problem,' she said.

'A friend of mine burnt his house to the ground frying sausages,' he said.

'You're quite safe, I'm making toast.'

Sensing he was not welcome, he turned to leave, and then made a final offer. 'If you need a hand to rearrange the furniture just knock me up.'

Daisy was calm but threatening. 'Go away.'

'Right . . . right . . .'

As she closed the door on him, the toaster ejected a flaming love letter into the air. She stamped the flames out and continued her rampage against anything belonging to Sebastian.

Archie returned a third time. Daisy answered the door wielding the brush. Not a word was spoken but he got the message that she was in no mood to be bothered by him and scuttled off.

Moments later, the doorbell rang again.

Daisy flung the door open, intent on strangling Archie. But it was Franklin. He was taken aback by the venomous welcome.

'I brought your portfolio, minus Celeste's portrait, which was perfect by the way. I didn't think you'd want it.' He looked into the apartment. 'Except for a bonfire.'

She invited him in.

'Did you know?' she said.

He shook his head. 'The engagement came as a shock to me too. It won't last.'

'I really trusted him.'

'Apparently the staff knew about the affair for the past year.'

'He's been two–timing me for a year? A year! I assumed they'd started the fling in Italy.'

He handed her a key and a piece of paper. 'This is the key to my cottage in Cornwall. Get away from London for a while. Let things blow over.'

She didn't want to accept the key. He placed it down on the table. 'I'll leave it here, with the address, in case you change your mind. It would do you good. I know you don't have any family in London —'

'Or friends I can trust,' she said. 'Two–faced, backstabbing bastards!'

'You should get away for a while. I won't tell anyone, especially Sebastian, where you are. Mrs Lemon keeps an eye on the cottage for me. You can stay as long as you want.'

After Franklin left, Daisy decided to go out. She walked alone in the city, thinking about what had happened, wondering what to do. Finally, she returned home and went to bed.

It was 1am and she couldn't sleep. She checked her mobile phone for messages. Nothing. She switched it off and threw it on a chair. It could rot there. Everyone who had her number, apart from Franklin, had betrayed her.

She wandered through to the lounge, saw the keys to the cottage and decided to pack her bags. She put the bags in her car and drove off into the night.

Later, a road sign indicated — Cornwall.

The dawn was rising as she reached the small coastal town where Franklin's cottage was located. It was a picturesque area, comprising of a main street with shops, and cottages dotted around the outskirts.

A turquoise sea glittered in the distance. She stopped to find directions. The only person up and about was Sharky the baker.

He got out of his van to give her directions. He was about the same age as Daisy and twice the size; not fat, just big and brawny. His baker's whites were clean and tidy, though his hat barely contained his thick brown hair.

She showed him the piece of paper. 'I'm looking for this address.'

'Franklin's place — on holiday are you?'

'Is his cottage near here?'

'Right over there,' he said. 'The one with the fancy blue shutters and tacky crazy paving at the bottom of the hill.'

'Something tells me you don't like him.'

'Au contraire, Franklin's great. I just don't like what he's done with the cottage. We tend to speak our minds down here. Blunt but honest.'

'Then you won't mind if I thank you and then drive on because I'm in no mood to chat to anyone.'

She went to drive off, but he leaned on the car and tried to establish a conversation. 'Insulting but honest — good try. Keep working on it.'

She noticed the logo, SHARKY THE BAKER, emblazoned across the side of his van.

'Thanks again for your help, Sharky.'

'Anytime, sorry I didn't catch your name.'

She drove away without giving him any other information.

'Secretive city type,' he said. 'I love a challenge.'

Daisy parked her car outside Franklin's cottage. It was set slightly apart from several others that were dotted around. The garden was well kept with a small lawn, rose bushes and a colourful selection of flowers alongside the crazy paving. Although it was barely dawn, a neighbour, Mrs Lemon, was already up and spying on Daisy from her window.

Other curtains twitched, noting the newcomer's arrival.

Oblivious to being the target of several sets of eyeballs, Daisy took her luggage inside. The interior was comfortably furnished in shades of cream, with a traditional log fireplace in the front lounge. The kitchen opened out on to the back garden and had a window that she imagined would let in plenty of sunlight. Numerous photographs hung in the hall, mainly of Franklin and various friends who had stayed at the cottage. One photograph showed Franklin and Sebastian smiling together. She gave an involuntary growl at the rat.

By now, both Mrs Lemon and her daughter, Karen, were spying on Daisy, furtively peering out of their living room window with a pair of binoculars. Karen was aged early twenties, a modern and attractive brunette. Mrs Lemon tended the cottage for Franklin and decided to phone him about the strange young woman who appeared to have moved in.

Franklin was asleep in bed, alone, when the phone rang. 'Hello?' he said sleepily.

Mrs Lemon was brusque. 'A strange young woman has moved into your cottage. She has keys!'

'Daisy is a friend of mine, Mrs Lemon. She'll be staying at the cottage for a while. I want you to see to it that she gets everything she needs.'

'Oh, like that is it?' Her tone was laced with innuendo.

'No, it's not like that,' he said calmly. For some odd reason her harsh manner had never annoyed him. In fact, he often wished she would work in his London office. A bit like hiring a verbal rottweiler. On days when the printers were indeed shitting shoe horns, she would be an asset.

'What I'm going to tell you is strictly confidential,' he said. 'This goes no further than you and me.' He went on to confide the details of Daisy's situation with Sebastian.

Mrs Lemon couldn't wait to tell every juicy detail to her daughter. 'That weasel Sebastian has ditched his girlfriend, Daisy, and got engaged to Celeste.'

'Franklin must be delighted at the prospect of having Sebastian as a son–in–law,' Karen said dryly.

Mrs Lemon picked up the binoculars and spied on Daisy who was busy rummaging in the boot of her car. 'He's taken pity on the girl and is letting her stay at his cottage. He's always been a soft touch for a sob story.'

Karen took a turn at the binoculars. She watched Daisy collecting another bag from her car. 'What did you say her name was?'

'Daisy. She's an artist from London and works for Franklin. Apparently Sebastian had been diddling about with Celeste behind her back for over a year.'

Karen studied Daisy. 'She doesn't look like Sebastian's type.'

Mrs Lemon gave her daughter a knowing nudge. 'Another one bites the dust.'

'I dated Sebastian twice, TWICE.'

Mrs Lemon grabbed back the binoculars and hung them by the strap around her neck. 'Three times if you count the fiasco at the village fayre.'

'You should have been a mathematician, mother. You're obsessed with numbers.'

'And everyone watching you from the bric–a–brac stall.'

Karen sighed. 'Must you keep bringing that up?'

Their conversation was interrupted when they saw the tall, broad–shouldered figure of Jake Wolfe walking past their house. Jake, who was in his early thirties, owned the town's health food shop and was a local celebrity author. Karen worked for him as a shop assistant and had an occasional crush on her boss. He just missed being chocolate box handsome, and had sexy dark hair with silky strands that fell casually over his forehead, despite his attempts to sweep it back. His eyes were aquamarine blue, and Karen blamed them for the effect he had on her — along with his sexy smile.

Mrs Lemon pulled Karen back from the window. 'Get back, get back, I don't want Jake to see us being nosey.'

They were too late. Jake caught a glimpse of Mrs Lemon.

'Damn, he's seen me! Quick, Karen, pass me a duster.'

Karen grabbed the nearest equivalent — a cloth from an armchair.

Mrs Lemon snatched the cloth, slung her binoculars around so they hung down her back out of sight, and made a blatant show of polishing the inside of her front window. She waved at Jake. He nodded politely and walked on.

As Jake walked away, they saw Daisy lock up her car and go into the cottage. He didn't even notice her.

Mrs Lemon and Karen looked at Daisy, then at Jake — and exchanged a knowing look.

'Daisy must be devastated . . . heart broken,' said Karen.

'That would be interfering,' said Mrs Lemon.

11

Karen smiled. 'Wouldn't it.'

Daisy had fallen asleep on the comfy sofa. Nothing was unpacked. A sketch pad and pen were lying on a table, her artist's case was open, and a cartoon drawing of a horrible looking rat was stuck on the picture in the hall covering Sebastian's face. Franklin could still be seen smiling.

By mid day in the Cornish town, gossip was circulating about Daisy's arrival. Mrs Lemon had told them everything. Each person had passed on the gossip to another. The gossip trail led to Jake Wolfe's health food shop situated across the street from Sharky the baker.

Jake's shop was bright, quaint, and heavily stocked with products. Karen was wearing her shop assistant's outfit and was talking to Jake's uncle, Woolley, about Daisy and Sebastian. Although Woolley was retired, he still helped Jake with the business.

'This girl Daisy is staying at Franklin's cottage you say?' said Woolley, chewing over the gossip.

'Yes, and by the looks of her, she's really broken hearted — if you know what I'm getting at,' said Karen, winking at him.

'Jake's cure for love?' said Woolley.

Karen nodded. 'She'd be an ideal guinea–pig.'

Woolley was thoughtful. 'She's a city girl. She could be perfect.'

Sharky, who was in the shop buying liquorice, joined in their conversation with a barbed remark aimed at Karen. 'I thought you'd be ideal, Karen, considering you've got a crush on Jake and he's not interested in you.'

Karen glared at Sharky.

'Oh, I forgot, maybe you're still pining for Sebastian,' he said. 'You must have fond memories from the fayre, especially when you got to twirl his tombola.'

'I'm not pining for any man, especially a rat like Sebastian — or a half–arsed baker who thinks he can win me over with the promise of a custard flan.'

While they bickered, Woolley continued his original line of thought. 'This new city girl could be ideal. Does Jake know she's here?'

'Jake's blinkered to everything except his work,' said Sharky. 'Someone's going to have to tell him.'

Karen looked at Woolley. 'You're his uncle.'

'No, it's best coming from someone who's seen her. Jake will ask me what she's like and I've never met her,' said Woolley.

'She's cute, and pretty intelligent I'd say,' Sharky announced.

'You've met her?' said Karen, sounding surprised.

'Uh–huh! And I like her, but gut instinct tells me she's trouble — and I'm never wrong.'

Chapter Two

Whisky and a pork pie

Twilight shaded Franklin's cottage in deep blues and purple. Far off in the distance grey clouds moved in from the sea bringing a rainstorm with them.

Despite the weather, Sharky was in a jovial mood. He didn't think he had a snowball's chance in a frying pan of impressing Daisy. He was a realist. But even realists enjoy flirting and fanciful gestures. He sometimes wondered if perhaps fate would have an off day and he'd actually win the girl. Wouldn't that be a novelty.

Carrying an armful of bakery goods and fresh milk, he knocked on the door.

Daisy was asleep on the sofa, sprawled out like a rag doll that had been cast aside for a more glamorous model.

Sharky knocked on the door again.

She woke with a start, her eyes stinging and crimson from weeping in her sleep. She looked at the time on the clock and realised she'd slept right through the day. 'Triple shite!'

Her clothes were dishevelled as she went to the door. Whoever it was would have to take her at her crumpled best. It was only when she padded along the hall that she noticed she was wearing two different coloured socks — one pink, one yellow.

Sharky smiled warmly at her as if her unkempt persona was just fine by him.

'I brought some groceries — fresh bread, milk, sticky buns . . . the buns come with a warning — they're completely addictive.' The buns had white icing topped with sprinkles and a cherry. They looked delicious.

'Thanks, that was very thoughtful of you.' She reached for her purse on the hall table to pay him but he wouldn't hear of it.

He'd been hoping she would invite him in but she didn't.

'I thought you might need something to eat as you've slept right through the day.'

'I haven't,' she said. 'I've been . . . working.'

He eyed her ruffled appearance and didn't believe her.

14

'Any idea how long you'll be staying in Cornwall?'

She shook her head. 'I'm in two minds what to do.'

He looked down at her socks. 'Clearly.'

She'd seen the day she'd have bothered that her socks were odd, but perhaps her fashion buds had been numbed by Sebastian's betrayal because she really didn't care.

'Would you like to have dinner sometime?' he said.

'No.'

'Good to see you're practising the blunt but honest tack.' He leaned closer. 'Though we both know you've been sleeping all day.'

'I'm an artist. I was dreaming about my creative work.'

'I dream I'm tall, rich and handsome, but that doesn't help me bake the fresh rolls at 4am every morning.'

She looked him up and down. 'You're tall enough, own your own business and, well . . . you can't have everything.'

Sharky laughed. 'It's great to see you haven't lost your sense of humour.' He walked away and then said over his shoulder, 'They say laughter is the best glue to mend a broken heart.'

She closed the door and pondered his remark. Why would he say a thing like that? No one here knew her business.

Still fuzzy headed, she went through to the kitchen and put the groceries on the table, wondering whether or not to eat the food he'd brought. After a few moments consideration, hunger got the better of her.

Cupping a mug of hot, sweet tea with plenty of creamy milk, her mind replayed the incident when she'd punched Celeste on the nose. Oh how she wished she'd done it harder instead of by mistake. And to think of the hours she'd spent trying to get her nose perfect for the painting.

She took a gulp of tea to help swallow the rage that was stuck in her throat.

Stuff Celeste's nose! Her nose was perfectly straight. It was the rest of her that was twisted. But not half as twisted as Sebastian. How could he have duped her for a year? Where had she gone wrong? She'd suspected something wasn't right a few times, but he'd said she was being paranoid.

She bit into a sticky bun. How had he managed to persuade her to even think she was paranoid? But of course, Sebastian was so adept at the art of persuasion.

15

Twilight became night as she gazed out the window, lost in thoughts of harsh regret, watching the rainstorm, wishing she'd done things differently.

Waves of nostalgia threatened to drown her self–esteem but she kept bobbing to the surface like a champagne cork, fighting to see the world for what it was. Rather like the stripes on that little bumblebee, everything felt surreal, the wrong way round. She should be wearing the diamond engagement ring and marrying Sebastian, and Celeste should be sitting in Cornwall eating sticky buns. Though cakes probably never passed Celeste's lips. She was surprised anything passed those lips. Nothing seemed to please her. She had a mouth like a pussycat's arse — pursed tight when it wasn't happy. Now *that* was something she could have painted. Faces she was rubbish at, but a cat's backside depicting Celeste's pout would have got the full colour of her artist's palette.

She stared out the window at the stormy sky. How had she ended up in this despairing situation? Sitting in Cornwall like an abandoned waif gnawing the crumbs of a sticky bun was just plain wrong.

Realising her self–esteem was sinking fast, she put the brakes on her thoughts, and wandered through to the hall.

Seeing waterproofs and Wellington boots, she decided to try them on, having first hit the wellies on the floor to empty out any spiders, though there hadn't been a beady–eyed arachnid in sight.

Dressed for the rainy weather, she ventured out into the windswept night. No one else was about.

The large coat and hat drowned out her identity, and she savoured the freshness of the elements. She stretched out her arms and wished the wind would blow away the sorrow inside her.

Unfortunately the wind blew something else away . . . the contents of her pockets.

Jake Wolfe's house was situated on a hill overlooking Franklin's cottage and the town.

Jake sat in his study having dinner. His study was full of books, files, jars and various paraphernalia. He was single, successful and lived alone, apart from the numerous times when his uncle, Woolley, was there, like tonight. The town's health food shop was one of several shops belonging to Jake. He was also the author of herbal books. His latest book was his finest project involving years of research following on from the work of his late father to find the herbal cure for lovesickness. He believed he had found the cure for love. The missing key ingredient was a rare sea plant that was found off the coast of Cornwall. He had a few drops of the precious essence left, enough to test the latest version of his remedy which he believed was even more effective than the original mix. All he required was someone, preferably a young woman, who was at the height of broken heartedness, to test it.

Woolley poured himself a cup of tea. 'You don't usually listen to gossip, but a young woman, Daisy, is staying in Franklin's cottage. She works for him as an artist and he's given her the use of the cottage to get over the shock of being jilted by her boyfriend — Sebastian.'

'The arrogant, egomaniac who used to come down here for fishing trips with Franklin but got his tackle entangled in more women than he did in fresh mackerel?'

'The very fellow.'

'Never liked him.'

'Daisy thought Sebastian was going to marry her but he went off and got engaged to Franklin's daughter, Celeste.'

Jake sneered. 'They'll be the couple from hell.'

'And poor Daisy. Poor, *broken hearted city girl*.' Woolley looked at Jake waiting for the penny to drop.

Jake hurried over to the window and looked down at Franklin's cottage. 'Are you sure she was in love with Sebastian?'

'Yes, she's truly broken hearted. They'd been dating for two years, then . . .' Woolley demonstrated someone being kicked into orbit.

'Find out everything you can about her. I'll get the remedy ready.'

After Woolley left, Jake went over to the window again and gazed down at the cottage. Through the pouring rain he could see a light glowing inside. A few of the women in town had dallied with Sebastian, but he was curious to know what Daisy was like and what peculiar gap in her nature had attracted her to Sebastian's smooth as rancid butter charms.

Daisy was attempting to climb in an open window at the side of Franklin's cottage. The rain poured down, and she slipped and became snagged up in the roses.

Woolley saw her and went over to help.

'Need a hand?'

'I've locked myself out,' she said, trying to unravel her coat from the bushes. 'The wind blew everything out of my coat pockets including the key. I couldn't find it in the long grass in the dark.'

He pulled her free but they both stumbled back and ended up splattered in mud from a huge puddle in the garden.

'Think you could have another go at climbing through the window?' he said.

'Yes.'

He didn't doubt it. Any woman who could date Sebastian for two years had to have buckets of gumption.

Daisy wrestled with her coat, finally taking it off, and the hat, and throwing them down on the grass. She was soaked anyway and she could wriggle better without them.

'My name's Woolley,' he said, helping her to climb up. 'Woolley Wolfe.'

'You're not a bogus burglar are you?' she said, almost standing on him to reach the window.

'Nah, you're quite safe. I'm harmless'.

'It wasn't my safety I was bothered about — it was yours. I've had a horrible day . . . two days . . . I unintentionally skipped today and I'm on the edge of an outburst of vileness.'

'I've avoided marriage like the plague.'

'What?'

'Love, it'll do that to you — warp your brain and drive you bananas.'

She lost a wellie trying to squeeze through the window.

'Oops, your wellie's too big for you.' He shoved it back on to her foot.

'Thank you,' she said, and scrambled head first through the window, all dignity cast to the wind.

Some rumbling inside the cottage was followed by the front door being opened.

Woolley picked up the coat and hat from the grass, shook some of the mud off and took them round to Daisy.

'Do you want to come in and clean yourself up?' she said.

He shook his head and she could see raindrops and damp leaves from the bushes dangling off his beard. 'My nephew, Jake Wolfe, lives in the house on the hill.' He pointed towards the house. 'I'll go up there. Don't want to leave a puddle in your hall.'

He began walking away and then turned to her. 'Jake would love to meet you. I'm sure he could sort you out. He's a bit of a genius.'

He waved and walked on, bracing himself against the downpour.

'A genius at what?'

His voice was blown away by the gusts of wind. She couldn't decipher his answer.

'Sort me out?' she said, closing the door against the raging elements.

Woolley arrived back at Jake's house.

'Daisy locked herself out of the cottage. I gave her a leg up to get in through a window.'

'How does she feel?'

'Eh . . . quite trim, not too heavy — some of the weight was in her big wellies.'

Jake sighed in exasperation. 'No, does she seem upset, heart broken?'

'Oh eh . . . hard to say. She was blonde though. Definitely not Sebastian's type.'

Jake searched through his files for his research charts. 'What personality type is she?'

Woolley hesitated.

'Come on, Woolley, you're good at judging character.'

'Determined, angry, thoughtful and rather wild.'

'Strong but vulnerable — if it works on her I'll have found the ideal remedy.'

Daisy went into the town next day, having found the key to the cottage. Although she'd made an effort to tidy herself up she still felt like the walking wounded.

The locals watched her as she walked down the main street. She was aware of them looking but assumed it was because she was a newcomer.

The local postman, Mr Greenie, smiled at her. 'Cheer up, there's plenty of fish in the ocean.' He walked on.

Mr Greenie was the town's electrician, handyman/gardener, fire chief and various other professions. None of the jobs required his full–time attention so he wore different hats for each job.

Daisy wondered about his remark but couldn't make sense of it.

The day was bright and fresh, washed clean with the previous night's downpour. The town's main street was filled with small, bustling shops that looked picturesque in the sunlight. She walked past Jake Wolfe's health food shop and saw a sign in the window. She stopped to read it.

Broken hearted?

Feeling blue?

Come inside…

We have natural remedies for you.

Jake Wolfe noticed the attractive blonde outside the window. He watched her reading the sign. Being a small town it was easy to tell a newcomer. She had to be Daisy.

Daisy's curiosity was triggered. She certainly felt miserable. The idea of a natural pick–me–up appealed to her. What harm would it do to go in and have a look at what was on offer? She stepped inside.

Karen was working in the shop and went to approach Daisy.

Jake cut in.

'We need more strawberry jellies,' he said to Karen.

Karen stomped off to get them from the stockroom at the back of the shop.

Jake watched Daisy browsing for a few moments. She was far more attractive than he'd imagined, and it threw his senses slightly causing him to be over zealous.

'Can I help you?' he said, taking in her natural beauty. Her skin was pale and soft, and even without a scrap of make–up it looked lovely. She tucked a long strand of silky blonde hair behind one ear, unintentionally emphasising her sensual features. She wore grey jeans and a short sleeve white blouse that he thought suited her perfectly.

She hardly paid him any notice. 'Just browsing.'

Where would the natural remedy be she wondered looking around the shelves packed full of enticing products. She didn't want to ask about the remedy. She just wanted to read what was on the label. It had to have a label surely. Most items in the shop had three.

Then she saw a framed editorial feature from a newspaper showing Jake Wolfe and his herbal remedies. She remembered the name. He was Woolley's nephew.

Jake pursued her. 'I assumed you were interested in my cure for love.'

'Excuse me?' she said, looking up into possibly the most gorgeous blue eyes she'd ever seen. His sculptured cheekbones gave his face a classic, handsome appearance, and she couldn't see any family likeness between him and fuzzy whiskered Woolley.

'I saw you reading the sign in the window.'

'What sign?' she said, in no mood to feel pressured. She wished she'd worn her heels instead of flat shoes because his six–foot stature wouldn't have seemed so dominant.

'The sign you were reading — broken hearted, feeling blue, come inside, we have natural remedies for you.' His tone was deep and accusing.

'You're mistaken,' she said, and walked away thinking — arrogant arse.

Jake went after her. 'I can help. I've been working on a herbal cure for lovesickness. The remedy is ready for someone to test it.'

'I said you're mistaken. I only came in to buy . . .' she searched for a likely product. 'Some herb tea.' She picked up a packet of tea.

She could almost hear his brain calculating his next move as she headed for the front counter to pay for the tea with the intention of then making a bolt for it.

Jake followed her.

'Look, whatever Sebastian did to upset you —'

Daisy almost dropped the packet of tea. 'You know Sebastian?'

'Yes, and when I heard about your predicament I thought you would be ideal to test my cure for lovesickness, especially as you're from London. City girls tend to react differently to things than country girls, probably because their pace of life is faster, everything's more intense.'

'That's nonsense.'

'Perhaps it is, but if I could study you, I'd be able to find out. We've had some despondent holidaymakers here from the city of course, but they soon start enjoying themselves. Cornwall is like that. It's good for relaxing, good for the soul. But you're here to hide from Sebastian and what happened to you. You're the most miserable young woman we've had here in ages.'

Upset, confused and stressed out, her first instinct was to run, so she did, dropping the tea on the shop counter.

Jake hurried after her into the street and grabbed hold of her arm.

She pulled away from him, but his grip was strong, stronger than Sebastian's and she started to wriggle wildly.

'I apologise,' he said, managing to deal with her wriggling. 'I shouldn't have been so . . . so . . .'

'Overbearing, arrogant and blunt,' she shouted. Her face flushed bright pink and rage welled up inside her. 'Let go of me.'

He let go of her. 'I admit I have a tendency to be blunt but my offer is genuine.'

'Who the hell do you think you are talking about my private affairs as if it were headline news?'

'Small towns tend to gossip about newcomers,' he said.

'Oh well, that makes it all right then, doesn't it?'

'Franklin told Mrs Lemon why you were here and the story got bantered about a little. When she saw you moving into the cottage she phoned him and he let slip about Sebastian ditching you horribly.'

Daisy blinked at his tactless remark. 'You're blaming Franklin?'

'No, Mrs Lemon shouldn't have divulged a confidence, but she's renowned as the local busy–body.'

Karen hurried out of the shop. 'Don't you talk about my mother like that, especially to a stranger,' she said, her glossy dark ponytail swishing like a cat's tail.

'I'm not a stranger,' said Daisy. 'I'm the miserable, broken hearted city girl who is staying in Franklin's cottage and got ditched horribly by Sebastian. Apparently everyone in town knows my entire life story!'

'Yes, I know.' Karen dismissed Daisy's remarks as common knowledge and seemed more intent on arguing with Jake.

Sharky the baker was within earshot, having heard the verbal fisticuffs from across the street in his bakery shop.

'If you ask me, Sebastian must be crazy, stupid or both,' said Sharky. 'No man in his right mind would want to marry Celeste. She came into my bakery shop a few months ago to sample my raspberry torte. What a fiasco that was. Sebastian hasn't an inkling when it comes to women.'

'Isn't that a bit like the pot calling the kettle black?' Karen said to Sharky.

Sharky took the bait. 'You're just miffed because you can't get your claws into Jake.'

Karen glared at him. 'And your nose is out of joint that I'm not interested in you!'

Woolley and Mrs Lemon approached from nearby shops and joined in the fray. Woolley gave Daisy a smile of acknowledgement and introduced her to Mrs Lemon. In the sunlight, Daisy thought he looked even fuzzier than she'd imagined, and Mrs Lemon had features sharp enough to clip a hedge. Her mousy hair was pulled back in a bun.

'I asked Karen out once, *once* — as a bet,' Sharky said to Daisy.

Karen was outraged. 'I was a bet? Whose bet?'

Woolley intervened, preventing Sharky from revealing the truth.

'Right,' Woolley said, trying to sound sensible, 'that'll do. No need to drag up the past.'

Jake's eyes squinted at his uncle. Instinct told him the old rascal had been involved in the bet.

'You made a bet with Sharky?' Jake said to Woolley.

Woolley gave Jake a furtive look. 'Not really a bet, more like a . . .'

'Dare,' said Sharky.

Karen was insulted, and it took a lot to insult Karen.

Daisy listened to their bizarre antics. In these wild moments she almost forgot about Sebastian.

'I could tell you a few shockers about this lot,' Mrs Lemon said to Daisy. 'No wonder the women in this town have to rely on romance novels.'

Sharky mocked Mrs Lemon. 'Oh Hugo, she sighed breathlessly, as he pressed his hard lips against the searing heat of her pulsating beauty.'

Mrs Lemon shook her head at Sharky. 'He hasn't a clue,' she said to Daisy. Then she said to him, 'The only bun you're ever likely to stuff in the oven is your sticky pastry.'

Woolley laughed.

Mrs Lemon turned on him. 'And you're past it. Sell–by–date 1956.'

Woolley was indignant. 'I'm retired.'

Mrs Lemon poked her nose into Woolley's face. 'You've always been past it.'

Jake smirked at Woolley.

Mrs Lemon looked at Jake. 'And as for you, Jake Wolfe, you sit up there in that big house of yours all alone with not a woman in sight, brewing your weird potions. Cure for love indeed. I've never heard anything so ridiculous, and ironic coming from a man who's never known true love.'

Jake went to protest but Mrs Lemon said to Daisy, 'He's too busy with his nose stuck in books and herbal hocus–pocus nonsense to have a steady girl.'

Woolley stepped forward in Jake's defence. 'Jake's had loads of women.'

Mrs Lemon folded her arms across her tightly buttoned coat. 'Name three.'

Woolley became flustered.

'Not a word,' Jake said to Woolley.

'The macaroon girl from Devon,' said Karen. 'Right little floozy.'

'I never touched her macaroons,' said Jake.

Although their antics had been distracting, Daisy started to feel overwhelmed.

They were all squabbling when Daisy cut in. 'What is wrong with you people? Don't you have anything better to do than gossip?'

They looked at each other in silence.

Daisy sighed. She'd had enough of them and walked away. As she left, she heard them arguing with each other again.

'Cornwall, big mistake,' Daisy said to herself. 'I should've stayed in London — it's quieter.'

'Mad as hatters the lot of them,' a man's deep voice said behind her as she crossed the street.

She spun around to see a gorgeous blond–haired man grinning casually at her. His hands were tucked into the pockets of his expensive jacket. She estimated he was around the same age and height as Jake Wolfe.

'It's a popular misconception,' he said, 'that rural life is tranquil. Personally, I go to the city when I want to get away from the chaos.' His smile lit up his attractive grey eyes.

Daisy smiled at him. Her face ached from too many hours crying and hardly a smile for the past three days.

'Roman Penhaligan,' he said, extending a strong, elegant hand.

Daisy went to introduce herself but hesitated. 'Is there any need for me to say who I am? Everyone seems to know all about me.'

'No one knows everything about anyone,' he said. 'We've all got secrets. But yes, I do know the gossip, Daisy. It's difficult to ignore it when it's relayed at full volume across the main street.'

There was a sense of calmness about him that she liked.

'I was hoping to stay in Cornwall for a little while but I don't know if I can stand it,' she said.

'Well if you manage to survive the craziness until the weekend, I'm having a party at my castle. You're welcome to join us.'

He had a castle? She hated being so impressed.

'It's just along the coast. You can't miss it. It's the only one with turrets,' he said with a smile, not sounding in the least bit big headed.

'If I survive the mayhem, I may take you up on your offer, though I'm not sure I'll be the cheeriest of company.'

He fixed her with a direct look. 'You don't need to be. Everyone will be dancing. Come along and let your hair down.'

Oh how tempting his offer sounded, but was she ready to let her hair down? It was too confusing a thought, especially as she was secretly seething mad at everyone knowing her business.

She watched Mr Penhaligan walk away and reflected on the gossip — and Jake Wolfe. She was angry at his attitude. He knew she was an emotional wreck, but all he was bothered about was his blasted remedy. He was possibly the most selfish man she'd ever met, and the competition for that category was fierce.

Later in the day Daisy sat by the coast sketching the scenery. From the hill she was on, she could see wild grass and patches of flowers that led down to a beautiful sandy shore. White waves rolled up over turquoise water and disappeared into the sand.

Woolley approached her. 'I thought I should redress the balance of the gossip. Mind if I sit down?'

He sat down beside her.

'You can't take back the things you've all said about me,' she said.

'No, but I can tell you a few snippets about us.'

'I'm really not interested in gossip.'

'At least let me explain about Jake and his cure for lovesickness.'

She continued sketching while Woolley talked.

'Jake's mother ran off when he was a boy. His father was heart broken, never got over her leaving. He was a herbalist, like Jake, and spent the rest of his life searching for a cure for love.'

Daisy glanced at him.

'Anyway, Jake now owns several health food shops and he's also written books. His latest book is all about the cure for love. Jake's a determined sort. He's spent years searching for a remedy. He means well, and he thinks he's found the cure for lovesickness. Now he's working on an improved version of the remedy.'

'I don't think there could ever be a cure for love.'

'Don't be too hasty to dismiss it. Love is a symptom of our emotions. Jake believes he can treat the symptoms and mend a broken heart.'

'So we could all choose who we wanted to love?'

'No, but we could get over being dumped a lot better. It's a cure for lovesickness, unrequited love.'

'Like a few glasses of whisky?' she said.

He smiled and leaned closer. 'Imagine if you could take a sip of the remedy and feel better about . . . not what Sebastian did to you . . . it's not a remedy for treachery, but what if you didn't feel any love for Sebastian ever again. Wouldn't that be worthwhile?'

'It's tempting, but . . . is the remedy any good? Has Jake really found the cure?'

'He believes so. The special ingredient is a very rare sea plant that's found off the Cornish coast. Jake dives for it every year. Sometimes he finds it, sometimes not. Depends on the tides. He's got a tiny supply left, so it's not something to be wasted. He would like to use a couple of drops mixed into the remedy to gauge your reaction.'

'What's in the actual remedy?'

'Herbal essences matched to your emotions, such as jealousy, spite and paranoia.'

'Paranoia? I could have done with some of that when I was dating Sebastian. But then again, I was right to be suspicious.'

'Well Jake's got plenty of potions. He's always concocting stuff.'

'Surely there are plenty of women he can test his remedy on. Why me?'

'Because you're the only one who is on our doorstep right now — and you're from the city. He's tested the latest version on a few people in and around this area, but he's yet to test it on a city girl. He seems to think you'll have a different outlook being from a big city. Maybe this is true, we don't know. I also sense you're a decent sort who deserves to feel better about things.'

He got up to leave.

'You don't really know me,' she said.

'I know a good hearted young woman when I see one.'

He started to walk away.

'I set fire to Sebastian's love letters in the toaster,' she said.

Woolley smiled. 'Mrs Lemon tried to take my eye out with a knitting needle once.'

'You and Mrs Lemon were an item?'

'That's a secret. Even Jake doesn't know about her and me.'

He walked away.

'Many moons ago was it?' she said.

'Nah, a few months ago.'

'Did you take any of Jake's remedy?'

'No, I opted for the old–fashioned cure — whisky and a pork pie.'

Chapter Three

Love me forever

Daisy's nose was annoying her. Crying and sniffling had given her a nose as bright and shiny as a glace cherry. Rummaging through her make–up bag she found her trusty green concealer. Glamour was the last thing she was bothered about, but every time she caught sight of her nose it made her feel horrible, and she felt bad enough.

Dabbing the green cream on her nose, she waited for it dry while riffling through the contents of her make–up bag for a light foundation. She didn't usually wear a lot of make–up, mainly mascara and lipstick, but she had somehow accumulated more products to correct what was wrong with her face than to enhance what was right with it.

A loud knock on the cottage door jolted her senses. She zipped the bag shut, hurried through to the lounge and peeked through the net curtains. It was Jake Wolfe. She looked at the clock — almost 7pm. What did he want? Another go at her perhaps? Bring it on Jake!

Dressed in black trousers and a top, she tightened the hair clasp on her loosely gathered ponytail and went to answer the door.

Jake stepped into the hallway, his height and shoulder width seeming to fill it. He wore an open neck blue shirt and navy trousers, and his hair was damp as if he'd just showered. 'I've come to apologise for any embarrassment caused . . . and to eh . . . invite you to have dinner.' He saw the rat cartoon stuck on Sebastian's face but made no comment. 'There's a nice little restaurant in town.'

'I have other plans for the evening.'

'Indeed?'

She could tell by his tone that he didn't believe her. Okay, so he was right, but maybe she could have had plans for the evening. Roman Pen–whatshisname had invited her to his castle, that's if she lasted until the weekend.

'You know where to find me if you happen to change your mind,' he said.

'Yes I do and no I won't.'

He glanced again at the cartoon of Sebastian the rat as he was leaving. He paused and ran an agitated hand through his dark hair, pushing the damp strands back from his forehead. They flopped forward again instantly.

'If you hate Sebastian, why don't you let me help you? If I were you, I'd take anything less than poison to get him out of my system.'

'I've had one man rip my emotions to shreds. I don't want another one tampering with them.' Blunt but honest; she was getting better at it.

He nodded and stepped outside.

'You've got a green nose, did you know that?' he said.

Damn, damn, damn!

'It's concealer,' she said trying to sound as if she knew perfectly well.

'It's not concealing your green nose.'

'I've got a red nose actually.'

'So you use green make–up to hide your red nose? Women's logic is it?'

'Yes, perhaps you can ask the girl from Devon to explain it to you the next time she tempts you with her macaroons.'

The sinewy muscles in his jaw twitched and he gulped down whatever biting comment was choking him.

Not another word was exchanged. He marched off and she slammed the door shut.

Jake was working in his study later that night. A plate of sandwiches lay untouched on the table. He was unsettled and couldn't concentrate on his work. He finally left the house in a determined mood. It was a cold summer evening but his blood was boiling from his earlier encounter with Daisy, giving him his own central heating.

Wearing silky pyjamas, Daisy wandered through to her bedroom in the cottage. It had a sumptuous double bed, and the window looked on to the back garden. She'd showered and towel dried her hair and was looking around for a socket to plug in her hairdryer.

Jake strode purposefully towards the cottage. The lights were on. He knew she was at home.

'Other plans for the evening indeed,' he muttered.

Daisy found a socket, plugged in the dryer and — BANG — blew the fuses. The cottage was thrown into darkness.

Jake saw the lights go out. He cursed and talked to himself as he headed along the path. 'Pretending you're out won't work with me.'

Daisy scrambled about in the dark searching for a light. She struck a match, lit a candle in the kitchen, and in the process burned her fingers.

Jake crept round the back of the cottage. 'If she can be sneaky so can I.'

Daisy saw the shadowy figure of a man near the kitchen window. She panicked, thinking it was a prowler and immediately started to crawl around on the floor to hide out of sight.

Jake saw her. 'Trying to outsmart me, eh?' He knocked on the window.

The man was trying to break in! She searched around for something to defend herself with. She tried three items before she selected the biggest — a stuffed fish which was mounted on the wall — a prize catch from one of Franklin's fishing trips. Clutching it by the tail she took a wild swipe. Yes this would do the trick.

By candlelight she crouched down in the hall and then seeing an emergency number on a notepad next to the phone, she called the police.

An elderly woman answered. She was the local telephone operator.

'I need the police,' Daisy whispered.

'Are you phoning from London? You don't sound as if you're from around here.'

'I'm staying in Cornwall. My name is Daisy —'

'Oh you're the young woman who's staying in Franklin's cottage.'

'Yes, but I need the police. There's a man prowling around outside.'

'We don't have many prowlers, dear.'

'I'm telling you he's sneaking about in the bushes.'

'Now don't get yourself into a tizzy. What happened?'

Daisy heard the man moving around outside.

'I don't have time to explain,' Daisy whispered.

'You'll have to speak up. I'm a bit deaf.'

'The lights in the cottage fused when I plugged in my hairdryer.'

'Oh then it's an electrician you need. Policemen don't fix fuses.'

'No you don't understand.'

The woman didn't listen to any further explanation and started to dial a number to contact the electrician.

'Just sit tight, Daisy. Mr Greenie the electrician will be there in a jiffy.'

'Listen, please call the police,' said Daisy.

The woman wasn't listening. 'Franklin's fuses are always blowing. If you stick one thing too many in your socket — bang! Just hold tight until Mr Greenie gets there.' The woman hung up.

Daisy huddled by the phone and flicked through other emergency telephone numbers listed in Franklin's notepad. One number read: *Police direct line for emergencies.*

Daisy dialled the number.

The same woman as before answered the call.

'Hello?'

'Is that the police?' Daisy whispered.

'You'll have to speak up. I'm a bit deaf.'

Daisy growled to herself and put the phone down.

Enraged, agitated and completely at the end of her tether, she decided to go outside and tackle the intruder herself.

'I'm just in the mood to beat someone about the head with a stuffed fish!'

In fighting mood, Daisy stalked the shadow outside the cottage. She saw the man lurking near the bushes, crept up behind him and beat him over the head with the fish.

She caused little damage, to the man or the fish, but Jake got such a fright he instinctively wrestled his attacker to the ground. Despite fighting him like a wildcat, he overpowered her and they ended up on the front lawn.

In the moonlight he saw it was Daisy and she recognised him.

He pinned her down, and she felt his muscular physique beneath the fabric of his shirt as their bodies touched. His face was inches away from hers. A shiver of excitement made her catch her breath, and for a moment she could almost believe he liked her. It was the first time those aqua eyes of his had looked at her and she hadn't felt like a potential guinea pig. Then again, he could've been distracted by her beautiful cleavage that was partly exposed due to the buttons on her pyjama jacket being undone.

Across the street Mrs Lemon and Karen were watching them.

31

'Quick, give me the binoculars,' said Mrs Lemon.

Karen handed them to her. 'What is Jake up to with her?'

'It's too dark. I can't see a thing.' Then she remembered. 'The night–sight binoculars.'

'They're in the cupboard,' said Karen, dashing off to fetch them.

'It's great what you can buy online,' said Mrs Lemon.

Karen gave her the night–sights.

Mrs Lemon focused on Daisy and Jake.

'They're rolling about on the lawn,' she said, sounding shocked. 'He's straddled on top of her.'

Karen grabbed the night–sights. From the awkward angle it looked like they were having sex.

Karen snarled. 'Bastard!'

Mrs Lemon snatched the night–sights. 'Oh would you look at that.'

Karen stepped back from the window. 'How dare he jump on that little floozy when he knows he can have me any time. How dare he!'

'Am I seeing things?' said Mrs Lemon, refocusing the sights. 'What are they doing with a big stuffed haddock?'

'Don't be naive mother. People use the weirdest things for . . . role playing.'

'And what role would Jake be playing? Moby Dick? I've seen enough.' She went to put the night–sights down when she noticed Mr Greenie arrive at the cottage.

'Wait a minute. What's Mr Greenie doing there at this time of night?' Mrs Lemon studied him. 'He's wearing his rubberised boots. The fuses must have blown again.'

Mr Greenie approached Daisy and Jake in the front garden. He was carrying a toolbox. 'I've come to fix the fuses,' he said with a smile, not bothered that they were getting up from the lawn.

The three of them went inside the cottage.

Daisy thought the electrician looked familiar. Where had she seen him before?

Mr Greenie worked by torchlight at the fuse box to fix the fault.

Daisy and Jake sat by candlelight in the living room. There was a strange calm, as if nothing in the world was urgent.

'I shouldn't have hit you with the cod,' she said to Jake.

'Haddock.'

Daisy blinked.

'It's a haddock, not a cod,' he said, suddenly feeling like an idiot for mentioning it.

'Well, whatever it is, I shouldn't have battered you with it. I'm sort of strung out at the moment. I thought you were a prowler.'

'Do you usually attack prowlers?'

'Only if I've had a bad day, and I've had three of them.'

'I'm sorry about wrestling you to the ground. You caught me off guard. I saw the lights go off and thought you were pretending you were out.'

'The hairdryer blew the fuses.' She touched her hair. It felt like it was sticking up like a troll's bouffant. 'My hair must look a mess.'

'Tousled,' Jake said tactfully.

'It's been wild, windswept and tousled since . . . Sebastian ditched me horribly. Isn't that what you said?'

Jake looked guilty. 'Have you had time to think what you're going to do about Sebastian?'

'No. Franklin thought a break from London would do me good. Enjoy the quiet tranquillity of Cornwall.' She smiled. 'I haven't had a moment since I arrived here. It's been sheer mayhem and madness.'

'At least you haven't been dwelling on Sebastian and Celeste.'

Daisy sighed and looked at the candle on the table. 'I do wonder what they're doing. Right now they're probably having a romantic candlelit dinner. Sebastian liked that.'

Sebastian and Celeste were having a candlelit dinner.

Celeste shouted at him. 'I don't have to put up with your shit, Sebastian.'

'Fine,' he said. 'Frankly I'm bored with you. I must have been mad to give up Daisy. What was I thinking?'

He grabbed his coat.

Celeste screeched at him. 'She won't have you back, not after what you did to her.'

Sebastian turned and glared. 'Don't bet on it.'

Celeste threw one of the dinner plates. It missed him and hit off the door as he left.

Daisy sighed again. 'Sebastian was always so romantic.'

'Romantic perhaps, but he's a slimy liar. You can never trust a liar,' said Jake.

'I sometimes tell white lies. Does that make me untrustworthy?'

'White lies are allowed, sparingly of course.'

'I'm practising being blunt but honest,' she said.

'Ah, you've been talking to Sharky.'

'He's strangely likable.'

Jake's expression deepened. 'I suppose I'm not.'

'You bring out the worst in me. Do you have a remedy for that?'

'No, and I don't have a remedy for foolishness either. Sebastian must be a complete fool. If a woman like you was in love with me, I'd never dream of betraying her.'

'Ta–da!' said Mr Greenie as he switched on the lights.

The intimacy of the conversation was broken. Daisy blew out the candles and seemed slightly awkward about the situation. She wasn't sure why. Perhaps she'd said too much to Jake? Perhaps he had? She preferred it when they were fighting, even if it was a mildly sexy wrestling match. Fighting was straightforward. You knew where you stood. Her emotions were unsteady enough without Jake Wolfe tipping the balance.

Sharky arrived at the cottage. He walked in, curious about what was going on. He had another parcel of baking and flowers for Daisy. He spoke as if he was expected.

'Full house, Daisy? I thought we'd be alone.'

Jake glared at her. 'So you did have plans for the evening. A date with Sharky. Quick work for someone supposedly upset at being jilted.'

'You've got it all wrong,' said Daisy.

'Have I?' Jake said, and stormed off.

Sharky gave Daisy the flowers. 'What's up his arse?'

'Bad timing,' she said.

'Remember, policemen don't fix fuses,' Mr Greenie said to Daisy.

Daisy exchanged a look with Sharky as Mr Greenie smiled and bounded off.

'Don't even try to figure him out,' Sharky said to her.

Mrs Lemon and Karen were watching everything. The sequence of events made Daisy look flighty.

'That young woman is a brazen little floozy,' said Mrs Lemon.

'If Sebastian could see her now,' said Karen.

'He doesn't know she's here.'

'Is that right?' Karen said, with a sly smile.

'You can't keep turning up like this,' Daisy said to Sharky.

'Can't blame a man for trying. Speaking of which, Jake seemed jealous as he stormed off. I think he likes you.'

'He barely knows me.'

'Neither do I, but I like you. And I'm shallow. Jake has depth so he really must think you're special.'

'He's only interested in me as a guinea pig for his remedy.'

'Was that a scratch on his nose?' said Sharky.

'I thought he was a prowler.'

Sharky's eyes sparkled. A wild woman, eh? Oh yes, he loved that. Savouring those secret thoughts he gave her the parcel of rolls, cakes and buns. 'Remember what they say — revenge is the best revenge.'

'Don't you mean success is the best revenge?'

'No, I read it in a women's magazine. It definitely said revenge was the best revenge. Success takes time but revenge is the shorter and sweeter route. And speaking of sweet, I've popped a few buns in for you. Sticky buns are great with a glass of milk when you can't sleep.'

Daisy smiled. Her face didn't ache so bad.

When Sharky left, she looked up the hill at Jake Wolfe's house. How strange her world had become. It seemed like a million miles away from London . . . and Sebastian.

It was 2am. Jake Wolfe was in bed but he couldn't sleep. Daisy had unsettled him.

He got up and went through to his study to work. He read over the notes on his theory for the cure for love.

Various bottles of tonics sat on a shelf. The labels offered a selection of potions. ANXIETY. DESPERATION. PARANOIA.

Despite the selection, Jake opted for a bottle of whisky. As he poured himself a small measure, Woolley turned up at the house and joined him in a drink.

'I couldn't sleep' said Woolley. 'I saw your lights were on.'

'I was reading over some notes.'

'I thought perhaps Daisy was getting to you?'

'Nonsense.'

'Sharky thought you sounded jealous,' said Woolley.

'Suddenly the baker is a psychologist.'

'He didn't have a date with Daisy. He was just making a nuisance of himself.'

'There's a novelty,' said Jake.

Woolley sipped his drink. 'Why won't Daisy test your remedy? It's harmless. She's got nothing to lose.'

'When I asked her she mentioned about not wanting another man tampering with her emotions . . . or something like that. You know how women's brains work.'

'Oh that any man knows how women's brains work,' said Woolley. 'We'll have to persuade her for her own good. She's far too nice to be pining over a rat like Sebastian.'

'How are we going to do that? She's too stubborn.'

'I have a plan,' said Woolley, with a twinkle in his eye.

'No offence, but your plans have a tendency to backfire — badly.'

Woolley winked. 'This plan is foolproof.'

It was just after 2am. Daisy couldn't sleep. She sat at the kitchen window eating a sticky bun and drinking a glass of milk, gazing out at the night sky. Under other circumstances this would have been a beautiful evening. The cold, clear air gave her a spectacular view of the stars.

Lost in faraway thoughts, she remembered the last thing Sebastian had said to her in the park in London before flying off to Italy and effectively out of her life for good. No wonder a shadow of guilt had crossed his face.

'Anything else I can do for you?' she'd said to him.

'Yes, love me forever.'

Chapter Four

Gossip–free zone

'What's the foolproof plan?' Jake said to Woolley.

'You need an illustrator to do the herb and flower artwork for your new book. Daisy is an artist. She would be ideal for the job, and if she became involved in the project maybe she would be tempted to test the remedy.'

'I like that plan.'

Full of enthusiasm, Jake began assembling the chapters of his manuscript that he planned to show Daisy.

'In chapter one I need colour illustrations of melancholy thistle, fuchsia and heliotrope. No one ever seems to get my ragged robin right or my prickly poppy. I think I'll have to get them out and show them to her in detail.'

Woolley finished his drink while Jake searched through his vast collection of flower photographs.

'Perhaps she could do the cover illustration too,' Jake said brightly. 'I'd like an image of the blue flower emblazoned across the front and the Cornish sea in the background.'

Rummaging through his archives, Jake found one of his favourite photographs, taken by Woolley, when they'd gone diving off the coast the previous summer in search of the elusive blue flower. Woolley hadn't actually dived, but as a hardy old seaman he was in the water at the side of the boat helping and had taken the snap the moment Jake surfaced holding the flower. It was a happy picture full of sunshine and hope.

'Got a name for the flower yet?' Woolley said, studying the picture.

'No, it doesn't have a history. We'll probably have to name it ourselves.'

'Blue something or other?'

'I was thinking we could name it after your precious old boat.'

Woolley was taken aback. 'What — Dreamless?'

Jake nodded. 'I thought we could give it our history. I always liked that name.'

Woolley smiled. 'Dreamless it is.'

Jake looked at the time. It was after 3am.

Woolley gazed out the window. 'We're not the only ones up at this hour.' The lights were still on in Franklin's cottage.

'Daisy had a green nose today,' said Jake. 'Sebastian has a lot to answer for.'

'I'd love to see her get back on her feet and punch that blighter's lights out. She's got gumption that girl.'

Jake rubbed the scratch on his nose. 'She whacked me hard enough with a stuffed fish, and is deceptively vicious when you wrestle her.'

'Let's make the plan work, Jake.'

Jake agreed, making a mental note to go easy on the wilful wildflowers and essence of spite.

Daisy went into the town the next day to pick up some shopping. Fresh groceries were at the top of her wanted list. Perhaps the sea air was getting to her, but she had a notion for a crispy salad, fish and new potatoes. She also intended to search for a shop that sold artist materials because she planned to paint later and had run out of several colours.

When she'd woken up in the morning after a few patchy hours of sleep, her first thought was to pack her bags, get in her car and drive back to London. Then she imagined what it would be like to arrive at her old apartment. It was probably still stinking of stale smoke from toasting Sebastian's letters and filled with a thousand memories. Her heart sank. She wasn't ready to go back, not yet. But she needed a plan, even if it was only a sketchy outline of how long she was going to stay in Cornwall. An afternoon's painting would clear her thoughts and help her decide. A plan always worked for her.

Lost in thought, she hadn't realised she'd walked past Jake Wolfe's health food shop. Blast! She'd meant to avoid it. She could feel his eyes boring into her and stepped up her pace.

'Can I talk to you, Daisy?' he said, hurrying to catch up with her. 'I apologise for my behaviour last night.'

She paused.

'I'd like to invite you to dinner.'

Daisy went to object but he continued.

'It would be a business meeting.'

'Business?'

'Strictly business I assure you. I think under the circumstances it would be more civilised to meet over dinner.'

She glared at him. 'What business would we have?'

'I'm writing a book and I need an illustrator.'

'I don't draw people,' she said.

'It would be flowers and herbs. Definitely not people. I believe floral artwork is your speciality.' He fixed her with a direct gaze. 'Will you at least consider my offer?'

'No strings attached?'

He clipped the air with his fingers. 'Nothing. And it would be quite a lucrative deal.'

Common sense flew out the window and she heard herself saying, 'I'll consider it provided Mrs Lemon and other gossips are nowhere near.'

'Dinner at my house then,' he said quickly before she changed her mind, forgetting one vital thing.

'You cook?' said Daisy, sounding surprised. The man didn't seem to have any streak of domesticity in his body. Maybe he wasn't completely brutish?

'I cook up a storm,' he announced with bravado, remembering he couldn't cook to save himself.

'All right,' Daisy agreed.

'Great. Shall we say eight o'clock at my house?'

'I'll be there. I'd need to see what you've been working on before I could decide whether I could accept the project,' she said with a warning.

'Of course.'

'And I hope you won't try to get me to test your cure.'

'I promise not to mention it.'

'Can you hear what they're saying?' Mrs Lemon said to Karen.

Karen was straining to listen from the door of the health food shop. 'Jake mentioned something about his book project.'

Mrs Lemon pursed her lips. 'Still trying to persuade her to swallow his ridiculous love cure.'

'I wish she'd just swig it down and then go home,' said Karen through very glossy cerise lips.

'What else is he saying?' said Mrs Lemon.

'I can't hear. He's too far away, but he's fiddling with his forelock. You know what that means,' said Karen.

Mrs Lemon nodded.

'Guilty,' they said in unison.

'Whatever he's telling her he's not being totally honest,' said Karen. 'Eighty per cent truth, ten per cent ulterior motive, ten per cent skulduggery, and five per cent lies.'

'That's five too many, Karen.'

'Oh stop being a stickler for sums mother.'

Daisy suddenly felt they were being watched. 'We'll talk later.'

'Yes, right. See you tonight,' he said.

'Watch out, here comes Jake,' Mrs Lemon whispered.

The two women darted back into the shop trying to look as though they were none the wiser about his conversation with Daisy.

'I'll have a packet of your aniseed balls,' said Mrs Lemon, handing over the money to Karen. 'And an ounce of coltsfoot and feverfew.'

And a dash of lizard's tongue, Jake thought to himself, avoiding making eye contact with her.

Woolley was at the back of the shop.

'I've made a breakthrough and a balls–up,' Jake confessed, sinking down on to a sack full of sesame seeds.

Woolley shook his head. 'What's the good news and what's the cock–up'?

Jake sighed heavily. 'Daisy has agreed to come to dinner tonight at my house.'

'Great.'

'There's only one problem. I told her I'm cooking dinner.'

Woolley almost choked at the thought of it. 'You can't cook to save yourself.'

'Those were my thoughts exactly, but it slipped out before I could strangle my tongue. I'm no good at this devious malarkey.'

'What are you going to do?' said Woolley.

'Perhaps you could rustle up something?'

'I'm a worse cook than you. I can't even make toast without burning it.'

'You said you could survive in the jungle, living off creepy–crawly things you'd hunt in the bushes.'

'Only if I had Mrs Lemon along with me to cook the dinner.' He became thoughtful. 'I bet a woman like her could survive in the worst and most dangerous jungle.'

'I don't doubt it,' said Jake.

'Get Mrs Lemon to cook a meal for the two of you,' Woolley suggested.

'I can't. I promised Daisy that dinner would be a gossip–free zone. I gave my word. I made a promise and I intend keeping it.'

'You've only one other option…' said Woolley.

With an enormous sigh and gritted teeth, Jake got up from the sack and walked out of the shop across the street to Sharky the bakers.

Sharky was busy behind the counter wrapping flaky pastry. The shop was small but well stocked with a tempting selection of fresh baked bread, cakes, scones and sticky buns that smelled delicious.

Jake was the only customer. It almost choked him to ask for Sharky's help but he did it anyway.

'I've come to ask a favour.'

'A favour? What would the successful Jake Wolfe need from me?'

'When you think about it, it's really a favour for Daisy.'

'Okay, spit it out.'

'I've a business meeting with Daisy tonight at my house and I've sort of promised I'd cook dinner.'

Sharky laughed like a demon.

Jake continued, 'I've also promised that Mrs Lemon and other busybodies wouldn't know anything about it.'

'So you can't ask Mrs Lemon to whip you up a treat,' said Sharky enjoying every grimace on Jake's face.

'No, and Woolley is useless, so that just leaves —'

'The bastard baker.'

'Exactly,' said Jake.

'Okay I'll do it — if only to save you from poisoning Daisy.'

'Nothing too complicated.'

'Basically a heat it and eat it job?' said Sharky.

'How difficult can it be?'

Sharky sank Jake with a look and then selected a main course from the array of pies on sale.

41

'Let's see . . . a tasty savoury pie for the main course.' He handed the pie to Jake. 'And I'll bake something special for the pudding.'

'Dinner's at eight.'

'I'll bring it up to the house in plenty of time.'

Jake was holding the pie and looking a bit lost.

'What would you recommend I do with this?'

'Don't tempt me, Jake,' Sharky said with a smirk. 'I'll write down the cooking instructions.'

Sharky scribbled on a paper bag.

'Heat it in the oven for twenty minutes at Gas Mark 7.' He glanced at Jake. 'Can you boil vegetables?'

The vacant look on Jake's face answered that question. Sharky scored out the vegetables on the list and wrote, 'Serve with a green salad and sautéed potatoes.'

'Sautéed potatoes?'

Sharky sighed in exasperation. 'I'll bring the potatoes. Leave everything to me. All you have to do is heat the pie, Jake, just the pie.'

Daisy was carrying two bags of groceries when she finally found an art supply shop. She went inside expecting it to have a smaller selection of products than the shops in the city, and was pleasantly surprised to find it was a treasure trove of arts and crafts products. There were watercolours galore, beads, embroidery threads, jewellery and candle making kits and fashionable fabrics. A few customers were milling around, browsing and chatting.

'Can I help you?' said the shop assistant.

'I'm looking for watercolour paints,' said Daisy, choosing several colours as she spoke.

'Let me know if you can't find what you're looking for,' the woman said with a smile.

Daisy found everything she needed, and a few extras. She could spend hours in a shop like this.

'You get a free polished gem gift with your purchases,' said the shop assistant, handing Daisy a shiny, light green gemstone about the size of the nail on her little finger. It was sealed inside a clear wrapper and a description was printed on the label.

'It's lovely,' said Daisy.

'A peridot is said to mend a broken heart,' the shop assistant told her.

Daisy didn't feel like getting angry that everyone knew about her. 'Does it work?'

'It's worth a try,' said the shop assistant.

'I'm not one for believing in superstitions and things like that but . . .' Daisy dropped the gemstone into her purse.

Mrs Lemon had come into the shop and overheard the last piece of conversation.

Leaving the shop, Daisy was pursued by Mrs Lemon.

'I don't know what type of nonsense Jake Wolfe has been filling your head with but be warned — the man is at it. He was fiddling with his forelock.'

'Thank you for the warning, Mrs Lemon, but I am quite capable of dealing with devious men.' She walked on.

'Oh yes, of course . . . that's why you're in Cornwall.'

Daisy stopped. 'Did Karen really have a fling with Sebastian?'

'Fling? Huh! More like a fumble at the fayre. Karen has no sense when it comes to men.'

'I suppose trying to poke a man's eye out with a knitting needle makes a lot of sense,' said Daisy.

Mrs Lemon's eyes narrowed. 'I'll pluck his whiskers out one by one,' she seethed.

'Don't worry, your secret is safe with me. I won't be telling anyone.'

'Why not?'

Daisy stepped closer. 'Because it's not right. It would cause nothing but trouble.' She walked on again.

For once in a long time Mrs Lemon was lost for a cutting remark.

'It's too bad you're not into superstitions and things like that, Daisy,' she called to her.

Daisy turned back. 'Why?'

'I'm having a get together at my house tonight. Mainly the girls having a laugh and some fun with the tea leaves.'

Daisy couldn't imagine Mrs Lemon laughing. It would almost be worth going just for the novelty of seeing her crack a smile.

'Unfortunately I've plans for this evening,' said Daisy.

'We don't meet until midnight, so if you're around then, pop across.'

Daisy acknowledged the offer and then hurried on.

Two invitations for a night out within the space of a single shopping trip. If only her social calendar in London had been as busy. Between her work and Sebastian there had been precious little time for nights out with friends, which was just as well because her so–called friends had morphed into two–faced traitors who'd smiled at her while knowing what Sebastian and Celeste had been up to for a year.

No doubt the gossip was flying around Franklin's company. She could imagine them picking over the bones of her relationship with Sebastian like verbal vultures. Where has Daisy gone? (Wouldn't you like to know). Is she coming back? (Too bloody right). Well . . . she planned to go back, someday . . .

Daisy went back to the cottage, had lunch, and then headed to the coast.

The breeze was filled with the fresh, salty scent of the wild Cornish sea. Blustery or not, she set up her paints and began to sketch the white crested waves and rugged coastline. In the distance she saw a castle and dug a pair of binoculars that she used when painting scenery out of her bag for a closer look. It had turrets and was very likely to be Roman Pen–whatshisname's place.

'Focus a bit more to the right and you'll see my private apartments,' a man's voice said behind her.

Daisy almost dropped the binoculars, and blushed bright pink.

'I'm flattered,' he said, smiling. He looked at her artwork. 'You have a talent.'

'Thank you,' she said modestly. 'The scenery here is gorgeous.'

He sat down on the grass and gazed out towards the sea. 'I've travelled all over the world, but I've yet to find anywhere to compare with it.' He looked again at her painting. 'I hope you'll include my castle in your painting. If you do, I'll buy it.'

He watched her paint an outline of the castle into the distant landscape. 'There, I'll paint it in detail later.'

'Love it.'

The wind blew through his blond hair and she couldn't help but notice how attractive he was.

'So, has this Sebastian chap tried to contact you, to win you back?'

'No, he's engaged to someone else.'

'More fool him.' He held her gaze, and she felt the warmth of his smile.

'What about you? Is there someone special in your life?' she said.

His expression took on a faraway look. 'There used to be, but that's over now.'

'What happened?'

'I've always had a problem with someone liking me for myself and not just for my money, my inheritance, the castle.'

She nearly blurted out that surely many women would love him for himself, especially with his looks. The castle would be a bonus. But he continued to explain.

'I met Daphne at a party in London. She worked as a secretary for an accountancy firm in the city. I fell in love with her the first time I saw her. As foolish as it sounds, I thought — I'd happily marry this girl tonight. Which isn't in my nature at all. Anyway, I lied to her. I told her I was an accountant. I thought it would give us something in common and it wasn't a particularly far–fetched lie as I'm a businessman who deals with accountants regularly in the city.'

Daisy nodded, encouraging him to continue.

'So that night I asked her out and we began dating. I fell for her more than I ever thought possible, and she was happy thinking I was an accountant. It became more difficult to tell her the truth. I didn't want to ruin everything. Then fate forced my hand when she began hinting about wanting to get married. Married to me. I had to tell her the truth. That I was filthy rich and lived in a castle with all the trappings that went with it.'

'What did she say?'

'She said she hated castles. They were creepy and she liked the modern world, the city, not the past, not heritage or history.' He paused and sighed. 'The one time a woman loved me for myself, I wasn't myself. She wanted a more settled life. She wanted the accountant in London, and that wasn't me. So we split up.'

'Her loss.'

'Not really. You see, she wanted a husband and a family, one that she would spend most nights with. I'm often away abroad on business. I have to travel, to maintain the business and keep the castle and grounds financially safe. It would've been fine at first just the two of us, but if we'd had children she'd have been left to look after them for weeks on end while I was away. In a nutshell, I wasn't the man for her.'

'What happened to her?'

'She got married recently. I didn't go as far as to spy on her with binoculars,' he said, giving Daisy a mischievous wink. 'But I did sit in my car opposite the church and saw her come out with her new husband, an accountant with the firm she works for. She looked beautiful. And happy.'

'I'm sorry it didn't work out for you.'

He stood up and brushed the grass from his expensive corduroy trousers. 'I'll let you get on with your artwork. And remember, that one's mine,' he said, pointing at the painting. 'Even if the castle comes out a bit wonky, or the turrets twirl the wrong way, I'll like it. I love how you've captured the energy and colour of the sea. It's quite beautiful. It gives me a great feeling just looking at it,' he said, focussing on her rather than the painting. 'Some things that aren't quite perfect are all the better for it.'

'I'll bring it with me to the castle,' she said.

His smile lit up his face. 'You're coming to the party?'

'Yes, I think I will,' she said, reflecting his wonderful smile.

'Marvellous. I'll mark you down for the first dance with me.'

Daisy laughed. 'What have I let myself in for?'

'An evening where you'll dance your socks off. I'll send a car for you around seven in time for the banquet at seven–thirty.'

'Banquet?'

'Sounds very grand, but when you see the main hall I think you'll agree that a finger buffet wouldn't do it justice.'

She watched him walk away, feeling quite excited about the party, but the sea breeze picked up speed and blew her easel over, and almost spilled the water on her artwork. It reminded her of the day in the park when Sebastian said he was going off to Italy. Perhaps it was a warning not to trust Mr Penhaligan? But she dismissed the thought, set her artwork back up and continued painting. She wanted to make sure she got his turrets right.

Chapter Five

The dinner date deal

Clothes were strewn all over Daisy's bedroom. She held up a flower print tea dress. No, it wasn't right either.

'This is ridiculous,' she muttered to herself. 'It doesn't matter what I wear for dinner. I don't need to impress Jake Wolfe.'

Regardless of what she said, there was doubt in her reflection when she looked at herself in the mirror.

She didn't know what to wear for her dinner date with Jake. Not that it was a date, she corrected herself. It was a business dinner. Strictly business. So why was she so nervous?

She raked through the clothes she'd brought with her to Cornwall. Clearly she hadn't been thinking straight. She'd packed four suitcases and several bags with various cocktail and evening dresses that had been hanging in her wardrobe. Life with Sebastian had merited she have plenty of going out gear. However, holed up in Cornwall, sparkly cocktail numbers were of little use. She hadn't packed enough casual clothes. Of course she had the clothes she went shopping in, and those for lounging around the cottage, but neither seemed right for a business dinner.

Time got the better of her. She made a snap decision to wear one of the cocktail dresses, a classy midnight blue dress. She ran a brush through her hair, stepped into a pair of court shoes, and added a flick of mascara and a slick of lipstick.

Trying not to feel flustered, she made her way up the hill to his house. In the distance she saw Mrs Lemon walking past Jake's house and to avoid being seen, Daisy sneaked round to the back door.

Through the kitchen window she saw Jake running around like a madman, reading Sharky's instructions aloud and hurrying up to get everything ready.

'Heat the pie in the oven, Gas Mark 7 for twenty minutes.'

Daisy secretly watched him, amused by his antics and the messy state of the kitchen.

Jake phoned Sharky.

'The pie's in the oven. It's almost done. Where's the pudding? She'll be here soon.'

'I'm on my way. Keep her amused. Give her nibbles until I get there,' said Sharky.

Jake hung up and started getting the dinner plates ready.

Daisy went round to the front of the house and knocked on the door, pretending she had just arrived.

Jake fastened the top button of his black shirt, tightened his grey silk tie, and feigned calm as he welcomed her in. Calm from the chaos in the kitchen and the effect she had on him when he saw her. She looked great. And sparkly. He invited her through to his study where a dining table was set.

'I thought we could have dinner in the study and discuss business at the same time.'

'Dinner smells delicious.'

Jake looked worried. 'Does it? I'll see if it's okay. Make yourself at home.'

Jake dashed into the kitchen, and then dashed back to the study.

'Hope you like savoury pie. And there's pudding too.'

'What type of pudding?' said Daisy.

Jake sounded unsure. 'Eh...um...chocolate...trifle.'

He hurried off again to the kitchen.

Jake burned his hands taking the pie out of the oven. He cursed and put it down on the kitchen table which had a plastic tablecloth on it.

Sharky drove up in his van and hurried up to the house with the food. He sneaked a peek at Daisy through the study window. Daisy saw him but pretended not to notice, and then he scampered round the back to the kitchen.

Sharky tapped on the window. Jake opened it.

He gave Jake the salad, sautéed potatoes, and a spectacular pudding. It looked nothing like a chocolate trifle.

'Thanks, I'll settle up with you later,' said Jake, and closed the window.

Sharky tapped on the window. Jake opened it again.

'Your tablecloth is melting,' Sharky said calmly.

There was more cursing from Jake as he burned himself lifting the pie off the table. He blew on his fingers to cool them down, and put the potatoes in the oven to keep them warm.

'Daisy looks hot in that sparkly dress,' said Sharky.

'I'll open a window when I go through to the study.'

Sharky shook his head and closed the window himself.

Daisy looked around the study and lifted up some jars of herbs and bottles of brightly coloured liquid including one labelled PARANOIA. There were photographs of Jake with his father and Woolley. Happy photographs.

The unfinished manuscript of his latest book lay open on the desk. She read the title page.

'The Cure for Love by Jake Wolfe.'

The way Daisy was standing in the study, she looked lovely, the light catching the gold in her blonde hair, and for a moment, Jake quietly admired her.

She caught the look of admiration in his eyes, which caused him to scurry off to the kitchen again.

Jake served up the pie, potatoes and salad.

'This looks wonderful,' she said, taking a bite of the savoury pie.

Jake smiled tightly. A pang of guilt ricocheted through him.

'I'll get right down to business,' he said. 'I need an illustrator to work on my book with me for the next two or three weeks.'

'Why don't you work with the illustrators who did the artwork on your other books?'

'Although my books are always well presented, the illustrations in the last two books weren't quite what I had in mind and the publishers advised me to work directly with a good artist. This book is special and I want the artwork right. You work with Franklin so you have to be one of the best. Would you accept the project?'

'I've always wanted to illustrate an entire book. I've only ever done bits and pieces of artwork for manuscripts.'

'So you'll do it?'

Daisy hesitated.

'Financially, it's a very lucrative offer. And you'd be able to stay here a little longer . . . stay out of Sebastian's way. Think of it as a fresh start.'

Daisy smiled. 'Working would certainly help take my mind off Sebastian. And the money would be handy.'

'Great, that's settled. I'll get the publishers to put you in the contract and make sure you receive a fair royalty deal for the artwork. If the book's a success you'll make enough money to have your own cottage in Cornwall. Then you'd never have to leave.'

Jake realised he'd said too much. Daisy avoided further intimacy by changing the subject.

'Did you say there was chocolate trifle?'

'Coming right up.'

Jake hurried to the kitchen and raked through the cupboards for chocolate.

Daisy called through to him. 'I love chocolate.'

'Chocolate lifts the mood. Great for a broken heart.'

Jake finally found a chocolate flake, broke it in two and stuck it in the pudding. He hurried through to the study with it.

'I'm impressed,' said Daisy, admiring the large summer pudding, decorated with brambles, blueberries and raspberries.

'Me too.'

She watched him serve up two man–size portions. 'Do you always do the cooking?'

'No, Mrs Lemon cooks for me and Woolley.'

'Woolley lives with you?'

Jake smiled. 'No, it just seems as if he does.'

She tasted the delicious pudding. 'So what about your remedy? Is it really complete? Have you found the cure for love?'

'This is something that's been years in the making. But yes, I do think I've found a cure for love. I've tested it on lots of people while I started writing the book, and I've recently tweaked the remedy to make it even better.'

'And that's why you wanted to test it out on me?'

'Yes, though I do believe it's ready.'

'What about you, Jake? Ever been in love? Ever had your heart broken?'

'No, I've never been involved that deeply. Mrs Lemon was right when she said I was too busy with my nose stuck in my work — not that I'd ever tell her that of course.'

'What about the macaroon girl from Devon? Was Mrs Lemon right about that? Or didn't you touch her macaroons?'

'The local gossip got it wrong about her. She'd been jilted by her boyfriend and was one of the people I tested the cure on last year. It only partially worked but I've heard she's dating someone else now, so maybe my cure helped her after all. She said it certainly made her see her ex in a truer light.'

'Sebastian was such a conniving rat. Why didn't I see that? You know, I did suspect there was something going on behind my back, but when I mentioned this to him he told me I was paranoid. If I'd known you then I'd have asked for a dose of your herbal cure for paranoia to show that I wasn't paranoid. Then I'd have sussed him out long ago before I got so deeply involved.'

'I've promised not to try and persuade you to take the remedy, so I can only suggest you keep busy and let time heal things.'

Daisy toyed with the pudding. 'This is nothing whatsoever like chocolate trifle.'

Jake looked guilty.

'It's delicious of course, but if I was the suspicious type, I'd think that someone else made it for you. Perhaps I should have some of that paranoia essence later?'

Jake smiled. He could see that she'd taken his lies lightly and didn't mind.

'Maybe I'd be better taking a few drops of lizard's tongue instead?' he said.

They both relaxed, and enjoyed eating their pudding.

'Woolley mentioned a rare sea plant that you found off the coast of Cornwall,' said Daisy.

'It's a key ingredient of the remedy. I've very little of the essence left.'

'Can you get any more?'

'Next month, perhaps, when the summer tides change. I'll go diving for it again.'

'What does the plant look like?'

'It's a beautiful turquoise blue sea flower. I'd like you to paint it for the front cover of the book.'

'I'll be back home in London next month.'

'Then I'll have to kidnap you and bring you back to Cornwall to paint it.'

Again, Jake realised he'd said too much and jumped to another topic. 'Are you going to Penhaligan's party at the castle? I hear he's invited you.'

'Yes, if I can find a full–length dress to wear. The party sounds so grand — a banquet and all.'

'The dress you're wearing tonight would look lovely,' he said.

'I hope you don't think I'm overdressed tonight,' she said, suddenly feeling self conscious. 'I packed the silliest things. Just grabbed whatever came to hand from my wardrobe the night I left London.' She paused. 'I chose this because it was a lesser sparkly cocktail dress.'

Jake laughed. 'You make it sound like some exotic bird.'

'I suppose I could wear a greater sparkly cocktail dress to the castle. What it lacks in length it makes up for in gold dazzle.'

'You'll be the belle of the ball. I hope I can have the first dance with you.'

'I've already promised that to Roman.'

'Ah, well, never mind.'

She could see that he did mind, though those aquamarine eyes of his tried to hide it.

He stood up from the table. 'I'd like to show you my ragged robin,' he said, going over to his desk. 'And other plants and herbs I'd like you to illustrate. I've also printed out some sample chapters from my book so you can get an idea of what type of artwork I need.'

She went over to his desk and he gave her photographs of the plants and herbs. She studied the pictures. 'There are plenty of detail in the photographs, but I prefer to draw from life. Do you have any of these in your garden?'

'Yes, all of them.' He led her through to the back of the house, opened up the patio doors and flicked on several lanterns in the garden that lit up the night. The summer evening sky was going down in a blaze of glory, and from the hill the house stood on, she saw the sea glistening in the distance. The hill never seemed very high when she looked up at it from the cottage, but the view from Jake's garden was spectacular. The garden itself was magnificent. Natural but not untamed; an old–fashioned garden with flowers, herbs and greenery.

Jake led the way along a stone path to a small swimming pool that was almost hidden within the garden.

'My father bought the house because of the garden. Woolley and I look after it now. I've kept it more or less in its original style. Of course, I added the pool. Being a swimmer it was my one indulgence.'

A swimmer? So that explained the lean, strong physique and broad shoulders. Not that she was looking. Well, okay, she was, but her emotions were all at sixes and sevens, and besides, few women wouldn't notice a man like Jake Wolfe.

'Do you have a garden in London?'

'No, I live in an apartment. No garden at all. Not even a pot plant. But there are lots of parks in the city and I go to those quite often. That's where I was the last time Sebastian . . .' she tailed off.

Jake's blue eyes urged her to continue.

'Before he flew off to Italy, before he got engaged to Celeste. I was painting in the middle of a London park. He always knew where to find me.'

'He doesn't know you're here though?'

'No, Franklin's kept that quiet. Not that Sebastian would want to come and get me.'

Jake fought the urge to put a comforting arm around her slender shoulders. She seemed lost, as if abandoned without hope of the man she loved coming to reclaim her and take her home. Until tonight, he hadn't really thought of her like that, and it saddened him to see the stress she was under.

'I'm sorry,' he said quietly.

The clearest green eyes he'd ever seen looked up at him. 'Thank you, Jake.'

He cleared his throat. 'Shall we go inside for coffee or some wine or brandy?'

'Yes,' she said, and followed him back into the study where he poured them both a drink.

'To a better future, Daisy,' he said, raising his glass.

She raised her glass and drank a sip of wine. Then she flicked through the sample chapters from Jake's manuscript.

'I've included a list of the herbs and flowers I'd like you to paint. Some of them are part of the remedy, some aren't, but they're mentioned in the book. It's basically a theoretical book, explaining the methods used to create the remedy and the theory behind it.'

'When do you want me to start on the artwork?'

'Right away, if possible.'

'I'll start tomorrow morning.' She checked the time on her watch. 'It's almost midnight. I really have to go.'

'What?' he said, smiling. 'Are you Cinderella? Will your dress turn to rags at midnight?'

Before she could reply, the cuckoo clock on the wall juddered into life and an ancient looking wooden cuckoo gave a half–hearted coo. The mechanism creaked, and the bird disappeared back into the clock.

'I keep meaning to oil him,' said Jake.

Daisy laughed, put her unfinished wine down and headed out of the study. 'Thanks for dinner.'

He opened the front door for her. 'I apologise for the ruse.'

She looked up at him. 'You're not telling lies about anything else are you? I'd hate to think that you'd offered me the illustrating work to persuade me to test your cure for love.'

He almost confessed everything. Almost. 'I have your best interests at heart, Daisy. And I apologise again for lying about the cooking. Next time I'll cook dinner for us myself.'

'If you're as adept at cooking as you are at lying, I suggest you let Sharky prepare the food again.'

'You're probably right.'

'Goodnight, Jake.'

Daisy made her way down the hill. She could feel Jake watching her, but she didn't look back.

At the bottom of the hill she saw the lights were on in Mrs Lemon's house and a few people were milling around inside. Should she go to a fortune telling evening with the girls, or go back to Franklin's cottage where she'd sit wide awake dwelling on Sebastian? No contest.

Chapter Six

Tea cups and tittle–tattle

Mrs Lemon was surprised to see Daisy and invited her in. 'You didn't need to get all dressed up,' said Mrs Lemon, eyeing Daisy's dress.

'I didn't. I had dinner at Jake Wolfe's house.'

Mrs Lemon's hairnet rose a couple of inches above her brow. 'Dinner? Who cooked it? Certainly not Jake himself.'

Sharky stood behind Mrs Lemon looking guilty. Daisy almost didn't recognise him at first because he wasn't wearing his bakers' whites. Instead, he wore a shirt and trousers in biscuit colours that really suited him, and had gelled his thick brown hair back, emphasising his strong features.

Daisy gave Sharky a knowing look. 'No, Jake sent out for something. Dinner was delivered by a caterer.'

Sharky gave Daisy the thumbs up.

Mrs Lemon tut–tutted. 'More money than sense. I'd have cooked dinner. I've been baking all day for tonight's get together. He could have had share of my vol–au–vents.'

'Jake knew you were busy and didn't want to give you any more unnecessary work,' Daisy said, crossing her fingers for telling a little white lie.

Mrs Lemon's hairnet settled back down to its original position. 'That was very thoughtful of him.' She sounded quite taken aback.

'The tea's brewed,' Karen called through to her mother from the living room.

'Come on, let's go through,' said Mrs Lemon.

A table was set in the living room with a large pot of tea in the middle. A knitted tea cosy kept it warm. Cups and saucers were at the ready, along with jugs of creamy milk and a bowl of sugar. Around a dozen women were seated there, chatting. Daisy was introduced to them, though they already knew who she was.

Mrs Lemon handed Daisy a plate. 'Help yourself,' she said, pointing to the selection of cakes, sandwiches and vol–au–vents.

Daisy chose a vol–au–vent while Mrs Lemon poured her a cup of tea.

'I thought this was a girls' night,' said Daisy.

'Sharky's not man enough to count,' said Karen.

'I supply the cakes and that's my ticket to join in,' said Sharky, taking no offence to Karen's comment.

Everyone was seated around the living room. Candles in coloured glass holders lit the room, adding to the party atmosphere.

'Right,' said Mrs Lemon. 'Who will we start with?' She looked straight at Daisy.

'What do I have to do?' Daisy said.

'Drink your tea, then hand the cup to me without looking into it,' said Mrs Lemon. 'I'll read what's in your tea leaves. Remember, this is just for fun.'

Daisy finished her tea, being careful not to drink the tea leaves. She gave the cup and saucer to Mrs Lemon who tipped the cup upside down on the saucer to drain the remainder of the tea and turned it three times clockwise before studying it with interest.

Everyone was quiet, waiting on Mrs Lemon's interpretation of the leaves. The tiny sequins in her hairnet sparkled in the light.

'I see the winds of change in your cup, Daisy. Everything scattered to the four corners of your cup.'

Daisy swallowed hard. She'd never had her fortune told, for fun or otherwise.

'I see a flower here in your cup, near the handle. And you're going to be tempted by a man who is not right for you. Three men are in the leaves.'

Daisy gasped. 'Three?'

Karen named two. 'Jake, Sebastian and —'

'Me,' said Sharky.

Mrs Lemon studied the leaves. 'Is there anyone else in London who has taken your fancy?'

'No. No one in London,' said Daisy.

'Strange,' said Mrs Lemon. 'There's definitely three.'

'Me,' Sharky said again.

Mrs Lemon focussed on the cup. 'All three of these men have made mistakes, or done you wrong. But only one of them is right for you. Not necessarily the one you think.'

Everyone was silent, wondering who these men could be.

Sharky was the first to break the silence.

'Anyone want another yum yum?' he said, offering a plate full of the special doughnuts.

'What about Sebastian?' said Karen. 'Is there anything else about him in Daisy's cup?'

Mrs Lemon turned the cup in all directions. 'What star sign is Sebastian?' she said to Daisy.

'He's on the cusp between snivelling rat and lying toad,' said Daisy.

'Yes, there he is. He's definitely one of the three. And I see a ring, but he's turned away from it. You know what that means,' said Mrs Lemon.

Daisy didn't, but most of the others did.

'The engagement's off,' said Karen.

'Are you sure?' said Daisy.

'No, but that's all I can see in your cup,' said Mrs Lemon.

Everyone was silent again.

'Can I tempt anyone with a custard finger?' said Sharky.

The evening continued with four of the women having their tea cups read.

Daisy listened, but her thoughts kept drifting to Sebastian. What if Mrs Lemon was right and the engagement was off?

At the end of the night, everyone headed home with a paper bag filled with leftover cakes and sandwiches. Daisy and Sharky were the last to leave.

'Are you going to Roman Penhaligan's party this weekend?' Mrs Lemon said to Daisy.

'Yes, why? Was there something in my cup about this?'

'I was trying to think who the third man could be,' said Mrs Lemon. 'Could it be Penhaligan?'

'I hope not,' said Karen. 'First Jake, then Roman. Will there be any eligible men left around here?'

'Me,' said Sharky. 'Besides, Mr Penhaligan's out of your league, Karen.'

Mrs Lemon's hackles rose. 'Nonsense. He's an eligible man, and Karen's a lovely young woman. Just because he's got money, it doesn't make him any better than her.'

Sharky backed down.

'I've no romantic interest in Mr Penhaligan,' said Daisy.

Mrs Lemon leaned close to Daisy. 'But does he have an interest in you?'

'I don't know, but we seem to get along quite well,' said Daisy.

'We'll find out at the party.' said Mrs Lemon.

Sharky opened the front door.

A light summer rain misted the evening air.

'I'll give you a lift to your cottage,' said Sharky. 'You don't want your lovely dress getting ruined in the rain.'

The cottage was in viewing distance, but Daisy took him up on his offer and climbed into the front passenger seat of his baker's van. They arrived in minutes and he parked outside her cottage.

'I still think I could be the third man in your cup,' said Sharky, turning off the engine.

A streetlamp lit up the van and she looked at Sharky in the light. Yes, he was a fine looking man, just not the man for her. At least she didn't think so.

'Remember, Mrs Lemon said that the three men have made mistakes, or done you wrong. But only one of them is right for you. Not necessarily the one you think.'

'You haven't done me wrong, Sharky.'

'I've been a nuisance and caused aggravation between you and Jake. But I'd never do you wrong, Daisy. Never. You can rely on me.'

'Thanks. I'd like us to become friends.'

'We *are* friends. You and me, Daisy. When all this hullabaloo with love and romance is done, we'll still be chewing over the gossip with a cup of tea and a sticky bun.'

She leaned over and gave him a huge hug. He had muscles like a bear and was a definite pleasure to cuddle, though she'd never give him the wrong impression. She wasn't physically attracted to Sharky, but her heart was certainly warming to him.

From the window of his house, Jake saw Daisy with Sharky and assumed she had a date with him.

'He could be giving her a lift,' said Woolley.

'At this time of night? It's after two in the morning. She should be in bed, asleep, not up at this hour.'

'We're up,' said Woolley.

'Yes, but we're . . . fervent.'

58

'Look, she's getting out of the van and going into the cottage. He's driving off.' Woolley glanced at the other cottages. 'Ah, the lights are on in Mrs Lemon's house. She must have been having one of her girls' nights.'

'Tea cups and tittle–tattle.'

'I'll ask Sharky what they were talking about.'

'Oh yes, I forgot, he's the only cock in the hen house. Buys his way in with buns.'

'I reckon Daisy was having her fortune told.'

'So that's why Cinderella was in such a rush to leave tonight.' Woolley frowned.

'Never mind. Find out what Mrs Lemon told her. Utter drivel obviously, but Daisy may be influenced by it.'

'Mrs Lemon has an uncanny knack for reading the tea cups. Don't underestimate her psychotic prowess.'

Jake couldn't be bothered correcting Woolley.

Woolley's eyes had a faraway look. 'She told me once that I would run naked along the shore with only a packet of biscuits covering my modesty.'

'That's hardly likely,' said Jake.

'Well . . . she was sort of right, but she was out by about twenty–years.'

Jake stared at his uncle. 'You streaked along the shore?'

'No, no, it wasn't like that. The lads and I were egging each other on to swim in the surf. I lost my trunks in the waves and my clothes got washed away. All that was left was the remains of our picnic, and I used a packet of chocolate biscuits to hide my particulars while I ran up the dunes to my cottage. But the point is, Mrs Lemon saw that in the tea leaves.'

59

Chapter Seven

Drink, dancing and scandalous gossip

Jake yawned and wandered through to the kitchen to get some breakfast. Bright sunlight shone through the yellow blinds giving a golden glow to the kitchen. He poured the last of the milk over his bowl of cereal, and then he noticed Daisy sitting painting in his garden beside a patch of wildflowers.

He went out to see her.

'I thought I'd make an early start,' she said. She'd already finished several watercolour illustrations.

'A late night and an early start. You're certainly burning the candle at both ends.' He made no attempt to disguise the accusation in his voice.

'Mrs Lemon had a party and it didn't start until midnight. Not that it's any of your business.'

'I'm sure Sharky and you had a great time.'

'So, you've been spying on me from your window.'

'I wouldn't call it spying. I just happened to be looking outside and saw you canoodling with the baker in his van.'

'Canoodling?' she said, almost choking back the laughter. 'Don't be ridiculous. There's nothing going on between Sharky and me. But why would it bother you if there was?'

'Ah there you are,' Woolley said to Jake, wandering into the garden. 'The big delivery has arrived at the shop.'

'I'll be right with you,' said Jake.

Woolley looked at one of Daisy's illustrations. 'I see you've got Jake's ragged robin right.'

Jake snapped out of argument mode and looked at her artwork. 'It's perfect.'

Woolley started to walk away. Jake followed then turned back to talk to Daisy.

'I'm sorry for what I said. And thank you for making a start on the artwork. Help yourself to whatever you need from the house — tea, coffee, anything.'

'Okay.'

'I'll see you later,' he said, and then hurried after Woolley.

Before he was out of view he looked back over his shoulder to see her watching him. He waved.

She waved back, wondering why he disturbed her so.

Jake's health food shop was busy. Mr Greenie, dressed as the Fire Chief, inspected the premises for the fire regulations. Jake and Woolley unpacked deliveries of products while Mr Greenie checked around the premises.

Mr Greenie adjusted a pile of boxes in the storeroom and then approached Jake and Woolley. 'Well done, Jake. Brilliant job.'

Jake frowned.

'It worked, eh?' said Mr Greenie.

'What worked?' said Woolley.

'Jake's cure for love. Daisy looked happy this morning when I saw her painting in the garden. She's well rid of Sebastian. It just shows you what a trip to Cornwall and a quirky potion can do for you.'

Jake tried to explain. 'But she hasn't actually taken the remedy —'

Mr Greenie didn't listen. He ticked a form on his clipboard and handed it to Jake.

'All the fire regulations are up to scratch in the shop. That's you hunky–dory. Must dash.'

Jake watched him leave the shop.

'I have to say, Daisy seems a lot stronger,' said Woolley. 'Sharky says she enjoyed Mrs Lemon's party and had her fortune read in the tea leaves. Apparently, there were three men in her cup. One of them was Sebastian, and one of them was you.'

'Me?'

'I think the two of you will work well together. And I thought perhaps she was starting to fall for you.'

Jake looked hopeful. 'You think so?'

Karen overheard their conversation. 'I'd say she likes Roman Penhaligan. He's certainly got his eye on her and they've been very chatty. It seems that quite a few men fancy her.'

Karen indicated towards the front of the shop. Daisy and Roman Penhaligan were talking outside.

'You'd better do something quick,' Woolley said to Jake.

'Daisy is still in the vulnerable rebound stage. The last thing she needs is to get involved with Penhaligan. What's he got that I haven't apart from a castle on the coast, a boat and an exciting lifestyle?'

'You'll have to pull out all the stops, Jake. Show her that you've got some pizzazz.'

'I've got plenty of pizzazz. Haven't I?' said Jake. 'What'll I do?'

'Have a party at your house. A real corker. Invite everyone,' said Woolley. 'And have it before his party.'

'I haven't had a party like that at the house in years. Perhaps never.'

'It's about time you did. But you'll need an excuse. You don't want everyone thinking you're desperate.'

Jake and Woolley racked their brains for a moment, and then Jake had an idea.

'The book! I've almost finished the manuscript. We'll have a party to celebrate that.'

Sharky was browsing at the treacle toffees and overheard them.

'Did someone say party?' said Sharky.

'Yes, I'm having a party at my house tonight. You're welcome to come along. Plenty of drink, dancing and scandalous gossip.'

'My kinda party,' said Sharky.

Jake called to Karen, knowing she'd been listening.

'You too, Karen, and tell Mrs Lemon.'

Roman Penhaligan came into the shop.

'Jake's having a wild party at his house tonight. Everyone's invited,' Karen said to Roman.

Roman looked at Jake. 'Wild party? Count me in.'

Jake smiled tightly.

Karen served Roman Penhaligan while Jake spoke to Woolley at the back of the shop.

'I was hoping he'd say no.'

'Never mind. We have to get this party organised,' said Woolley.

'Music. We'll need some good music,' said Jake.

'Leave that to me. I know just the person to ask.' Woolley went to approach Karen but Jake pulled him back.

'No, don't ask Karen. She'll revel in making me feel out of touch with things. She's been a bit waspish lately.'

'It wasn't Karen I was going to ask. It was Mrs Lemon. She's got all the latest hits.'

'Mrs Lemon?'

'Don't let the tweed coat and brown handbag fool you. Underneath that hairnet is a brunette bombshell.'

'I'll take your word for it,' said Jake.

'Seriously, after a couple of sweet sherries you should see her mambo,' said Woolley.

'I have no desire to ever see her mambo. I can't imagine Mrs Lemon shaking her booty.'

'I'll have you know that my mother may not be able to get her legs up in the air as high or as often as she used to, but she's won trophies for her can–can,' said Karen.

'I stand corrected,' said Jake.

Daisy came into the shop to buy fresh milk and began talking to Roman Penhaligan.

Jake approached them.

'What about you, Jake? Fancy coming to my party at the castle?'

'Yes, I'm planning to be there,' said Jake.

'Excellent. And I'm looking forward to your party. See you tonight.' Roman left the shop.

Daisy looked at Jake. 'Party?'

'Yes, I'm having a wild party at my house to eh . . . celebrate the manuscript being almost finished. You'll be there of course.'

Jake sounded edgy. Daisy was suspicious of his motives.

'Wouldn't miss it,' said Daisy.

'Good, good.'

'I didn't think you were the wild party type.'

'I might surprise you,' said Jake.

'You already did.'

The party at Jake's house that night was lively. Everyone was there except Daisy. A buffet, mini bar, DJ box and dance area were set up in a large room adjoining Jake's study. Mr Greenie was wearing his barman's waistcoat and seemed to be an expert at mixing cocktails. He was also doubling as the DJ.

Jake whispered anxiously to Woolley. 'Daisy's late. I hope she turns up.'

'She's a city girl. She's probably used to being fashionably late. We've only been jigging for half an hour. Give her time.'

Roman Penhaligan approached them. 'I've been looking for Daisy. I was hoping for a dance.'

'She's being fashionably late. Why don't you dance with Karen,' said Jake.

Roman smiled pleasantly and went over to ask Karen to dance.

'I've got a feeling that something's not right,' Jake said to Woolley.

'You really like her, don't you, Jake?' said Woolley.

'Ironic, isn't it. Just when I've almost perfected the cure for love, I'll end up needing it for myself. Daisy is probably still secretly pining for Sebastian.'

'Oh I think she's over him. I've seen how she looks at you. When she was sketching your hollyhocks this morning, I sensed the chemistry between the two of you.'

Jake was unsure. 'Roman Penhaligan seemed to be working his charms on her.'

'Nah, Daisy is just being friendly with him. You're needing a few drops of your paranoia. My money's on you, Jake.'

'Who are we betting on this time?' Sharky said to Woolley.

'No one,' said Woolley. 'What's that you're drinking?'

Sharky held up his cocktail glass. 'I've got a Banana Whopper.'

Mrs Lemon walked past carrying a glass of sweet sherry. 'Always bragging,' she said to Sharky.

Roman Penhaligan joined Jake, Woolley and Sharky. He was sipping a cocktail. 'Daisy really is quite late.'

'I'll go and see if she's on her way,' said Jake. He went into the adjoining study. He looked out the window and became despondent as there was no sign of her.

On a shelf were several bottles of herbal essence labelled — PARANOIA, SPITE, JEALOUSY and WILFUL ABANDON. He lifted the bottle of PARANOIA and took a few drops.

Sharky saw Jake taking the PARANOIA essence.

'It must be handy having all these concoctions. I've got to make do with a sticky bun and a mug of cocoa to make me feel better. Mind you, it works a treat.'

'If we could bottle it, we'd make a fortune,' said Jake.

'Your cure for love should be worth a mint.' Sharky looked at the manuscript on the desk. 'So you've finally finished it.'

'Almost. I've tested it on numerous people over the past few years, constantly adjusting it until it's as effective as possible. The theory's complete. I just need one final test before I send the manuscript away to the publishers.'

'Will readers be able to rustle up the remedy themselves?'

'No, but hopefully one day it'll lead to the product being made and sold. It all depends on whether people really want a cure for love.'

'Would you take it?' said Sharky.

'It depends on the woman. If I really loved her, and there was no chance that she cared about me, then yes. I'd have to be very sure that I wanted to wipe away all the feelings I had for her.'

Sharky nodded.

'Would you take it?' said Jake.

'Yes indee–dee. But no woman's driven me to despair yet. Daisy is lovely, but I was only ever flirting with her.'

Woolley came into the study.

'What about you, Woolley. Would you take the cure for love?' said Sharky.

'I've seen the day I would have, but a stiff drink and a night out with the lads usually did the trick. At least we used to pretend it did,' said Woolley.

Roman Penhaligan joined them in the study, and saw Jake's manuscript lying on the desk. 'Ah, is this the infamous book?'

Jake nodded.

'We've been discussing if we'd take the cure or not,' said Sharky.

'I certainly would if I needed it,' said Roman.

While they were discussing their disastrous love lives, Jake saw Daisy arrive. He brightened up and hurried to let her in. He had the bottle of PARANOIA in his hand. He was pleased to see her and helped her off with her coat. Her red cocktail dress sparkled under the lights. She appeared to be edgy.

'I'm sorry I'm late. I eh . . . I was going to lie and say that I'd fallen asleep but the truth is . . .' She hesitated and glanced at the bottle of PARANOIA. 'The truth is . . . I wasn't going to come to the party.'

'Why not?'

'Because I'm confused. Perhaps you've got a potion for that,' she said. 'I realised something when I'd changed my outfit five times, trying to decide what to wear. I asked myself — who was I trying to impress? I'm supposed to be broken hearted because of Sebastian, so why was I so keen to look good tonight? Why was it so important to me? And I just felt really unsure about everything.'

'Perhaps you wanted to look good for Roman Penhaligan?'

'I don't think so. Maybe I really should try some of your paranoia.'

Before they could talk further, Roman Penhaligan cut in.

'How about a cocktail instead?' Roman said to her. 'Mr Greenie is a whiz at mixing them.'

Roman encouraged Daisy to follow him to the bar. She glanced back at Jake as she walked away.

Jake grimaced. He'd missed his chance again to spend time with Daisy. He took a large swig of paranoia from the bottle.

Later, Jake sat on the sidelines of the party looking glum. Roman Penhaligan had monopolised Daisy.

Woolley and Sharky were sitting having a drink. Mr Greenie wore headphones and was giving it large in the DJ box.

'You'd better do something,' Sharky said to Woolley. 'Jake's making a complete arse of himself. It's obvious he's pissed off with Penhaligan.'

Woolley nodded.

Mr Greenie left the DJ box and hurried over to Woolley and Sharky.

'You'd better do something about Jake,' he said to them. 'He's acting like an arse. Want me to make a cocktail to liven him up a bit?'

'Yes, make it a corker,' said Woolley.

Mr Greenie hurried over to the bar and started mixing a cocktail.

'Why don't we give Jake a dose of his own remedies? He's got bottles of the stuff in his study for everything under the sun,' Sharky said to Woolley.

While Mr Greenie gave an entertaining display of cocktail mixing, Woolley went to the study and came back with a bottle labelled WILFUL ABANDON.

66

'If he doesn't drink the cocktail, I'll give him a couple of drops of this. It's very mild. Completely harmless,' said Woolley.

Sharky seemed interested in the remedy.

'Wilful abandon? I could do with some of that myself,' said Sharky.

'No way. You're incorrigible enough as it is,' said Woolley.

Mr Greenie came over with the cocktail. He handed the glass to Woolley. There was fine mist wafting from it.

'This is one of my specialities,' said Mr Greenie.

'What's in it?' said Woolley.

'What's not . . .?' said Mr Greenie.

Woolley took the cocktail over to Jake. 'Have some of this. It'll cheer you up.'

Jake took the glass, looked at it, and then put it down on the table beside him without drinking any of it.

'Thanks, but you know I'm not one for funny concoctions.'

'Is that right?' said Woolley.

Woolley put the bottle of WILFUL ABANDON down beside the cocktail glass.

'Nope. I've already had a dose of paranoia thanks.'

'Did it work?' said Woolley.

Jake shook his head. 'Remember it only works when the paranoia's unwarranted.' He indicated towards Daisy and Roman. 'Obviously I'm not paranoid. She really seems to like him.'

Woolley became angry. He whispered to Jake. 'Fight for her! Don't just sit there. This is your chance. That's what the ruddy party was for!'

The music became livelier. Mrs Lemon put her sherry aside and got up to dance. She was conservatively dressed, but she really could boogie. Woolley was mesmerised and left Jake so he could go to another part of the dance floor to get a better view of Mrs Lemon.

A few others got up to dance. Sharky asked Karen to dance and she accepted. Then Jake saw Roman Penhaligan getting up to dance with Daisy. She looked over at Jake, and then concentrated on dancing with Roman.

Jake watched them for a few moments, and in a fit of pique, he took a swig of the WILFUL ABANDON, straight from the bottle, and then drank the cocktail. He shuddered as it took effect. He was fine for a short time and then he got up to dance — on his own, which was just as well because no one was capable of keeping up with him.

Jake danced like a happy maniac. Everyone else, including Sharky and Karen, stepped back, giving him centre stage. Mr Greenie kept the music loud and lively to suit the mood. Daisy was speechless as she watched Jake's uninhibited performance.

'And there was me thinking he was a party pooper,' Roman said to Daisy.

Woolley, Sharky, Karen and Mrs Lemon were fascinated.

Karen admired Jake. 'I never thought he had it in him.'

Sharky started to compete with Jake. He wasn't quite as spectacular, but Karen seemed to enjoy it. Sharky shimmied over to her, enticing her to join him. 'Come on, Karen.'

Karen joined Sharky on the dance floor. Others started to join in again. The party really livened up.

'Shall we?' Woolley said to Mrs Lemon.

Mrs Lemon started dancing with Woolley.

'Don't worry. You can be snippy to me again tomorrow.'

Mrs Lemon almost smiled.

Daisy stood beside Roman Penhaligan watching everyone dancing. She seemed sad. Roman got hauled up to dance by Karen and Sharky, but Daisy stayed on the sidelines looking pensive. Moments later, she put her drink down and left quietly. No one noticed.

Jake and the others continued dancing.

The rainy night in London reflected Sebastian's mood. He paced up and down the lounge in his apartment and then phoned Franklin who was working late in his office at the publishing company.

'I've been trying to contact Daisy for days. She's switched her mobile off. You have to know where she is.'

'My lips are sealed. I promised I wouldn't tell anyone, especially you, Sebastian.'

Chapter Eight

The party at the castle

Sharky carried a board of freshly baked wholemeal loaves into the health food shop, and Mr Greenie, wearing his postman's uniform, delivered the mail to Karen.

'Is Jake not in yet, Karen? Hasn't quite gotten over the party, huh?' said Sharky, stacking the bread on a shelf.

'He phoned to say he'll be in later. I think he's wondering what he got up to last night. Woolley says Jake can't remember somersaulting across the dance floor,' said Karen.

Mr Greenie sounded chirpy. 'I've got it all on video. I'll give him a copy. It was quite a performance. If he hadn't been a health food aficionado, he'd have done well in the circus.'

Sharky laughed even though Mr Greenie was being straightforward.

'Jake looked quite buff with his shirt off. He's fitter than I thought,' said Karen.

'Whatever was in that cocktail certainly put some fire in his breeches,' said Sharky.

'One of my special concoctions will do that to a man,' said Mr Greenie.

'I loved your cocktails, Mr Greenie. I don't even have a hangover,' said Karen.

'I wonder what happened to Daisy? She left the party early,' said Sharky. 'I wish she'd stayed a while longer.'

Karen sighed huffily. 'Must be great to be popular. I wonder if I should be a blonde?'

'No, you suit being a mysterious brunette,' said Sharky.

'False flattery will get you nowhere.'

'I'm wearing her down,' Sharky said to Mr Greenie.

Karen glared at Sharky.

'Well, I'd better push on. I've got a couple of van loads of pies and pastries to deliver to the castle. Mr Penhaligan made a large order this year for his party, so I'll see you later. And remember, you promised me a dance,' Sharky said to Karen.

'I did no such thing,' Karen called after him.

Daisy picked up the painting she'd had framed at the art and craft shop. They'd done a wonderful job, and she intended taking it with her to the castle to give to Roman.

On the way back along the main street, she saw Karen and a few other women going in and out of a little boutique. A fairytale blue evening dress was on display in the front window, and the shop advertised the sale and hire of evening dresses and accessories. She rightly assumed the women were collecting their dresses for the party that night, and a spark of hope that there would be a dress she could wear made her go inside the shop.

Karen had a full–length black evening dress in clear wrapping draped carefully over her arms. She'd hired it for the night. Daisy saw that it had a few diamante gems on the straps, and thought it would suit Karen.

'If you're looking for a dress,' Karen said to Daisy, 'I don't think there's anything left. At least anything that's affordable.' Karen glanced at the shop owner, and let her explain.

'Yes, Karen's right. Almost everything's gone. All the hire wear and practically every dress we've got. Well . . . except the one in the window, though it's not really for sale here. It's one of our top designs. These go to our designer outlet in London. It's terribly expensive. We used it for our front display.'

'It's beautiful,' said Daisy, going over for a closer look. It seemed to be her size and the label confirmed this, but when she saw the price tag she almost gasped. It was definitely out of her price range. Not that she was hard up. Franklin paid top rates for her art, but most of that was used to pay for her apartment in London and her car. She wasn't in debt and had a bit of savings, but this would be too extravagant. Even the cocktail dresses she owned were found in bargain niche shops in the city.

'All the crystals and sequins are sewn on by hand,' said the woman, not trying to entice Daisy to buy, merely proud of the workmanship.

'It's exquisite,' said Daisy, admiring the pale blue chiffon skirt topped with a crystal encrusted bodice.

Three other women collected their hire dresses, a red satin temptress dress, glittering green ball gown, and a pink confection — every dress was lovely.

'I'm sorry there's nothing left for you,' the shop owner said.

Daisy thanked her and left the shop carrying the painting. She'd just have to wear a cocktail dress which would be fine. At least she had the painting framed for tonight.

Karen carried her dress into the health food shop and hung it up carefully at the back of the storeroom. Jake was serving at the counter and saw Daisy walking past on the other side of the street.

'That's me got my dress for tonight,' Karen said to Jake, then she noticed him watching Daisy. 'There were no dresses left for Daisy. But I'm sure she'll wear one of her sparkly numbers.'

'No dresses left at all?' said Jake. 'Surely there must be something. It's a dress shop.'

'All the women in town have hired every dress available, and the others have been bought,' said Karen. 'The shop's practically empty, except for the one in the window.'

'What's wrong with it?'

'Nothing, except the price. It's their top designer dress.'

'Did Daisy like it? Was it her size?'

'She certainly liked it and it would fit her, but it's far too expensive,' said Karen.

Jake left the shop immediately and came back ten minutes later with the dress packed in a huge box tied with ribbons.

Karen gasped. 'Oh my goodness, you bought it.'

Woolley was sorting stuff in the storeroom. Jake sat the box on the counter and went through to tell his uncle what he'd done.

'You paid how much?' Woolley shouted.

'You said I should fight for Daisy,' said Jake.

'Yes, but I was thinking more of boxes of chocolates, flowers, wining and dining her. Not that you can't afford to buy her the dress, Jake. You can. But wow — that's expensive.'

'Do you think she'll accept it? She won't be offended or anything. You know how women can be when it comes to clothes and shopping. I want to be sure before I go and give it to her.'

'I think she'll be as surprised as I am.'

'Right, I'll be back in about half an hour. Keep an eye on the shop,' said Jake.

Daisy was trying on her gold dress when Jake knocked on the door of the cottage. She opened it to find Jake holding the huge box, and stepped aside to let him bring it in.

'Before you say no, can I just give you this as a gesture to make up for all the stupid and argumentative things I've said since you came here,' he said, putting the box down in the hallway.

Daisy saw the label on the box. 'Is this the dress?' she said, unable to hide her excitement.

Jake smiled. 'I heard what happened.'

Daisy opened the lid of the box and saw the crystals sparkling in the hall light. 'Oh, Jake . . .'

'I have to get back to the shop,' he said, 'but I'll see you at the party tonight.'

He went to turn, but she instinctively wrapped her arms around him and gave him the biggest hug ever. For a second he held back, then he squeezed her tight and pulled her close to him, feeling the softness of her body under the liquid gold sequinned fabric.

'I don't know how to thank you, Jake,' she said, smiling up at him.

'Promise me the last dance tonight. Penhaligan has the first dance, but save the last one for me.'

She released her grasp, and stepped back before she was tempted to kiss him, and nodded.

He smiled at her again, and then headed back to the shop.

Daisy didn't know what to think. At first she chided herself for being so easily swayed by a beautiful dress, but then she thought that it was the fact that he'd done this for her. His kindness got to her. Jake didn't seem the type of man to do something like this. He'd gone against the grain of his nature just for her. Franklin had been kind, and Sharky generous with his supply of baking, but somehow Sharky seemed used to doing things like this. Jake didn't. Maybe her emotions were still raw and too close to the surface, but something felt different, as if a piece of the hurt from the past had been released never to return.

'I think it'll look great on you,' Sharky said to Jake in the health food shop.

Jake was working at the computer in the stockroom and looked up at him.

'Blue's definitely your colour, Jake. Have you got the sparkly stilettos to go with it?'

Jake pushed his chair back from the computer and gave a languid smile. 'Very funny,' he said to Sharky. 'I wondered how long it would take before everyone found out about me buying the dress.'

Sharky's hair stuck up in wild spikes and he had flour on his face and down the front of his bakers' whites. He was up to his eyeballs cooking the last load of pies and pastries for the castle order but had popped over just to poke fun at Jake.

'Sorry, Jake,' he said. 'I couldn't resist it.' He leaned into the storeroom and said in confidence, 'Honestly, I think that was very thoughtful of you.' He nodded, smiled, and then left Jake to get on with his work.

'Huh! It's all right for some women,' Karen said huffily and loud enough for Jake to hear. 'It cost me half a week's wages just to hire my dress and accessories.' She went back to serving at the counter, lips pursed tight.

Jake locked the shop up an hour early so that everyone had time to get ready for the evening.

Karen collected her black dress from the storeroom as Jake flicked the lights off and got the keys ready to lock up at the front. She picked up her handbag from the counter and noticed an envelope sitting on the till. It had her name on it.

'What's this?' she said to Jake.

He didn't answer and continued to lock up.

She opened the envelope and saw there was money inside.

'Enjoy the party, Karen.'

The smile she gave him lit up the shop. There was more than enough money to pay for the cost of her dress. It was the equivalent of another week's wages.

'Thank you,' she said, and gave him a quick hug, before hurrying away with her dress to start getting ready.

Jake smiled to himself. Two hugs within an afternoon. He must be doing something right.

'Are you coming over to have your hair done?' Mrs Lemon said to Daisy at the cottage.

'What?'

'Most of the girls wear their hair up for the party. We all do each others chignons. You can never get it right on your own.'

'An up–do?' Daisy said, thinking this would be perfect. 'I've never been able to put my hair up properly by myself.'

'Come on then,' Mrs Lemon beckoned, hurrying away and waving Daisy to follow her.

Daisy closed the cottage door, but didn't lock it. No one needed locked doors here. The telephone operator had been right. They didn't get many prowlers. She breathed a sigh. How easy it was to live in a place like this, if you could cope with the chaos and gossip, which she thought she was becoming more used to.

A man screaming and women laughing sounded from Mrs Lemon's house. Mrs Lemon adjusted her hairnet and hurried inside. Daisy followed her. The sun shone bright, promising a lovely, warm evening, and there was a feeling of excitement in the air.

In the living room several women had a man pinned to a chair. His flailing legs looked familiar, and then she saw it was Woolley.

'Let go of me,' he shouted, but was instantly silenced when Mrs Lemon took charge of the hair clippers.

'Keep still you old fool, or I'll have your nose off,' she said.

Without giving him time to breathe, she buzzed the clippers into action and within moments his nose hairs had been shorn.

'There,' said Mrs Lemon. 'Now off you go while we get our hair done.'

With his nose tickling him like mad, he scuttled away. Daisy noticed his beard had been trimmed and he was all spruced up, wearing caramel coloured trousers and a smart tweed jacket.

'Right, sit yourself down,' Mrs Lemon said to Daisy. 'What would you prefer — a chignon or a French plait?'

A vast array of hairspray, gel, clips and accessories were strewn around the living room which was packed with women of all ages, fixing each other's hair.

'I'm not sure,' said Daisy.

Leaving the women to decide what suited her, she ended up with a classic chignon that she was delighted with. A sprinkling of glittery clasps held it in place. Mrs Lemon gave her another blast with the hairspray.

As the time wore on, they started to put their make–up on. Karen was in charge of this, and Daisy had to admit that Karen had a talent for applying make–up.

Daisy ran back to Franklin's cottage to pick up her make–up bag and brought her dress, shoes and evening bag with her so she could get dressed at Mrs Lemon's house. All the women were getting ready together, and Daisy shared her silver and gold eye shadows with anyone who wanted them. Her vast selection of corrector items came in useful too as few of the women had anything like them. Her green concealer was particularly popular. Daisy helped apply it and advised how to add the necessary foundation. Everyone agreed the woman most improved was Mrs Lemon herself. The make–up softened her features and knocked years off her age. She even tried the gold eye shadow, though there wasn't a product in anyone's make–up bag to disguise her frequently pursed lips.

When they were all dressed and ready, they stood outside Mrs Lemon's house in the early evening sunlight. Mrs Lemon wore a flattering black and gold dress and jacket, and Karen was stunning in her chic black dress with her hair up to show off the diamante detail. The crystals on Daisy's blue chiffon dress glittered in the light and she enjoyed the heat of the evening sun on her bare shoulders.

Daisy, though, felt bad that a special car had been sent to pick her up.

'We've got our transport all arranged,' said Mrs Lemon.

As if on cue, a mini bus drove up and stopped outside her house.

'All aboard,' Mr Greenie said, dressed in his dinner suit but wearing his bus driver's hat.

'See you at the party,' Daisy said as she waved them off.

The classic car Roman Penhaligan sent for Daisy arrived on time. His butler drove it. The man, in his early sixties, opened the door for her and helped scoop her dress into the back seat. He also put the painting, which she'd carefully wrapped, beside him on the passenger seat.

'I must say, of all the ladies dresses I've seen in years, yours is one of the most beautiful.'

'Why thank you.'

'My pleasure. The castle's a short drive from here.'

The driveway up to the castle was just like Daisy had seen in films, only this was real. The lawns were immaculately cut, trees and bushes clipped worthy of a picture postcard, and the massive front doors were open wide.

The butler helped her from the car and offered to carry the painting in for her. She let him. Handling the dress and her own nervousness was enough.

Music filtered out of the doorway as she approached. Elegant music, but lively, adding to the party atmosphere.

The grandeur of the main hall was breathtaking. Roman was right. A finger buffet wouldn't have done it justice. Long tables were set with white linen and white and gold dinner services, silverware and white candles. The lighting was warm with various wall lights and chandeliers casting a glow on the dance floor. The size of the room was extraordinary, and was already filled with people. Everyone was dressed up to the nines. She'd never been to anything like this.

A huge fireplace, unlit, was set on one of the far walls, with patio doors on either side opening out on to the lawns. Fairy lights were draped around the patio, giving a fairytale feel to the night. The weather had decided to behave itself. It was one of those languid summer evenings where the sun burned amber gold and the sky took its time in darkening.

'Ah, there you are,' Roman said. He wore a suave grey dinner suit, white shirt and a silk cravat. 'You look beautiful,' he added, stepping back to admire her dress. 'The most beautiful woman in the room.' He kissed her lightly on both cheeks, and then wrapped her arm through his to give her the grand tour of the castle.

'What do you think?' he said as they stood at the bottom of the wide staircase.

'It's the loveliest castle I've ever seen. You're very fortunate to live here.'

'I am indeed,' he said, smiling deeply at her, and for a moment she thought he was going to lean in for a kiss.

His butler approached. 'The painting is ready, Sir.'

'Wonderful,' said Roman and without telling her what he'd done, he led her through to his private study. On the wall was her painting.

'I love it. It's so fresh and lovely,' he said, never taking his eyes off her, making her think the words were meant for her rather than the painting.

'I'm glad you like it,' she said, genuinely relieved that the frame she'd chosen stood up to the elegance of its surroundings.

'I can admire it when I'm working,' he said, again directing the comment at her.

For a second, she felt like an accessory, like a piece of art, a belonging, and she didn't like how that felt, but she brushed it aside and smiled at him.

'Dinner is about to be served, Sir,' the butler announced from the doorway.

Roman offered her his arm, and they walked together through to the main hall. He was seated at the head of the top table, and seated Daisy in pride of place right by him.

Numerous sets of eyeballs clocked this gesture. He'd more or less made his intent of claiming Daisy very obvious to everyone.

One pair of eyes stood out from all the others. The vivid blue eyes of Jake Wolfe. This was the first she'd seen him tonight. Her heart jolted, the way it used to when she'd first met Sebastian. She hadn't felt like that in a long time. Dressed in a black dinner suit, white shirt and grey silk tie, Jake was the most handsome she'd ever seen him. Handsome and sexy. A dangerous combination.

'Did you bring that dress with you from London?' Roman asked as the first course was served by what seemed like an army of waiters.

'Eh, no, it's from a shop in town.' She deliberately didn't elaborate.

Jake was seated at the top table but further down, diagonally at the opposite end. Her eyes flicked at him. Should she tell Roman that Jake bought the dress for her? She decided to say nothing.

Towards the end of the meal, couples started getting up to dance. A live band played in the corner. Roman stood up and escorted Daisy on to the centre of the dance floor where they waltzed around and around. The dress moved like a dream, and every now and then she caught Jake watching them. No, watching her, his face giving no indication of his thoughts. Perhaps it was patience she sensed in him. She'd promised the last dance of the night to him.

Sharky was the only man to tap Roman on the shoulder and request to intervene. Other men kept their distance, unwilling to interrupt the party's host when he was with the woman he clearly seemed infatuated with.

Daisy admitted to herself that Roman was great company, and his blond handsomeness affected her in so many ways. She liked him. She liked his stunning grey eyes and the way he invariably seemed to smile with warmth just at her. In contrast, Jake's blue eyes, though gorgeous, seemed more serious, as if he looked at her with the unfathomable depths of the ocean.

Again, her circumstances and the whole occasion, where she was, so far from her life in London, threatened to overwhelm her. How quickly her life had become something else. She mentally struggled to hold on to the woman she was, who she used to be, because soon she would be stepping back into her old world in the city, without Sebastian, but nonetheless she'd be home again in her apartment, working for Franklin, picking up the pieces and pushing on. When she looked back on her time in Cornwall, would this night, this grand night, feel like a fairytale? Would her broken heart be strong again?

'I'm so glad you came here tonight,' Roman said, holding her in his arms as they danced to a slow and romantic song.

'Excuse me, Sir,' his butler said. 'There's a phone call for you.'

They stopped dancing but Roman kept a hold of Daisy. 'No calls this evening. I don't care who it is or what —'

The butler fixed him with a knowing look. 'It's Daphne, Sir.'

Daisy felt Roman's hold on her loosen a little.

'Daphne?' he said.

'Yes, she's getting divorced and requests that you go to London immediately to comfort her.'

Roman frowned. 'Divorced? But she's not long married. What happened?'

'She caught her husband in a delicate position with his secretary in the office,' the butler said. 'She found his secretary . . . sharpening her husband's pencil for him.' The butler winked at Roman.

'Jeremy cheated on Daphne?' Roman sounded incredulous.

The butler nodded.

'But he's an accountant,' said Roman.

The butler shrugged.

By now, Roman had let go of Daisy. He still stood close enough to touch her, but she felt the distance between them widen.

Roman nodded at the butler, who went away to the study, and then he looked at Daisy. The expression on his face had changed, and any thought that she could be the one for him was lost. Roman loved Daphne. Despite the fact that she hated castles, the flame still burned deep within him. She knew that he would leave the party and drive off to London.

'I'm sorry,' he murmured, sounding genuine.

Daisy smiled. 'I hope everything works out for you this time.'

Roman took her hands in his and squeezed them tight. 'Thank you, Daisy.'

The last she saw of him he was getting into his car and driving off into the night, his cravat wafting in the breeze. Daisy stood on the porch and watched the car's tail lights disappear. She didn't feel sad, but she didn't feel happy either. She wasn't sure what she felt.

The biggest transformation of the night was Sharky, seated at another table along with Karen, Mrs Lemon and Woolley. The flour–covered baker with unkempt hair had morphed into a dinner suited gentleman. The last time he'd worn his black dinner suit, it had been a neat fit. Now it hung better. He'd lost some weight. Not through dieting, but through being so busy he'd shed several pounds.

With Karen wearing her slinky but sophisticated black dress, they looked like a well–matched couple, which surprised Karen more than anyone.

'Sharky's looking dapper,' Mrs Lemon whispered to her daughter.

'He's lost some weight.'

'I think the macaroon girl from Devon has her eye on him.'

Karen didn't expect the pang of jealousy she felt when she saw the macaroon girl, in her tight–fitting, bosom flaunting frock, sidling up to him. She pulled at his arm, encouraging him on to the dance floor. They laughed and joked and seemed to be enjoying themselves, much to the annoyance of Karen.

Jealousy bubbled up inside her. She hadn't imagined she'd be envious of the macaroon girl from Devon. Then there was Daisy being loved and lusted after by Jake and Roman. Even Sharky wanted to dance with her, and that's what tipped the balance. Karen slipped off to a quiet part of the castle and made a furtive phone call on her mobile to Sebastian. She knew she'd regret it later but being perfect wasn't in her nature.

'Daisy is in Cornwall?' Sebastian sounded surprised.

'Yes, she's living in Franklin's cottage. I thought you should know.'

'Perfect,' he said. 'She's not seeing anyone else is she?'

'The competition's hotting up. You'd better get down here,' said Karen.

'I'll be there tomorrow.' Then he added, 'I've split up with Celeste.'

'There's a shocker,' said Karen.

After phoning, Karen rejoined the party.

Mrs Lemon read the guilt on her daughter's face right away. 'What have you been up to?'

There was no point in trying to outfox her mother. 'I phoned Sebastian and told him Daisy was here.'

Mrs Lemon rocked back on her low heeled shoes. 'What have I told you about meddling?'

Karen looked down at the floor. 'I couldn't help it. I feel jealous and irritated. Daisy's got Jake and Roman running around after her, and now Sharky's in tow with that macaroon tart.'

'I couldn't eat another thing,' Woolley said, mishearing their conversation.

Mrs Lemon gave him a steely glare. 'I should've taken the clippers to your fuzzy ears as well.'

Sharky was still dancing with the macaroon girl from Devon.

There was no mistaking the jealousy in Karen's eyes. She aimed her emerald daggers straight at him.

Sharky thanked the girl for dancing with him, turned down her blatant offer to spend the night in her big double bed where she wanted to demonstrate how high she could bounce on the springy mattress. She couldn't even tempt him with the offer to reveal how she made her macaroons so luscious.

Sharky went over to Karen.

The last dance music began to play.

Without a word, Sharky offered his arm to Karen. She linked her arm through his and they stepped on to the dance floor.

Woolley was already dancing with Mrs Lemon.

Mr Greenie put down his violin and found a lady he'd always quite fancied to dance with.

Jake urgently looked around for Daisy, then he saw her standing outside on the patio.

'Can I have the pleasure?' he said, holding out his hand, hoping she'd accept.

She placed her hand in his, and blinked out of her faraway thoughts.

The music started up, a traditional, romantic medley, and the lighting dimmed just enough to accentuate the end of the evening.

Fireflies danced outside in the evening air, adding a magical quality to the night.

Jake took Daisy in his arms and they began to dance slowly to the music. His touch was warm, or was it the spark of having Jake so close to her that she felt? Her senses were heightened. The events of the night, from her fairytale arrival to Roman's departure, ensured that. Whatever happened, she was sure that this would be a special night. One for the memories. The night she would always remember.

'I can hear you thinking,' Jake whispered in her ear, his breath disturbingly sexy.

'I don't want to think any more tonight, Jake. I just want to dance in this beautiful dress . . . with you . . . and forget everything else.'

This was exactly what she wanted to do, and yet to hear herself say this to Jake, sounded like she was listening to herself from far away. Perhaps she was? Maybe if she pretended hard enough, she could forget she ever loved Sebastian, forget everything except these moments dancing under the crystal chandeliers with one of the most handsome men she'd ever known. But did she know Jake Wolfe? She hadn't known him long, and yet the short time she'd been here with these people who gossiped and knew each other's business, was the equivalent in time to months in London. In the city, there were people she'd been acquainted with for a while and knew far less about them, and their motives, than she did about Jake and the others.

'You're thinking again,' said Jake.

'Don't let me think,' she said, shaking her head as if to cast the thoughts aside. 'Do something, anything, to make me forget.'

If she'd had any notion that he'd pull her close and dance her off her feet then she'd have been wrong. He pulled her close all right, but then he kissed her, long and passionately yet lovingly. And she responded, without a care of what anyone thought of them. She kissed Jake Wolfe until she stopped thinking about everything except those moments with him. His lips were sensual and Jake could certainly kiss. For a man who sat up on the hill alone in his big house, Jake was a master at kissing, though why should she have expected any less from a man who had found the cure for love? Love and heartache and passion had been part of his life for years. It poured from him, all the love he was starting to feel for Daisy. The love he already felt.

And then he danced with her, and she laughed and smiled, and once again, a piece of the past, the hurt she'd endured, had gone.

'This makes my party last night dull in comparison,' Jake said.

'Oh, I don't know. Those bare–chested backflips of yours were impressive.'

A look of embarrassment crossed his face. 'I was hoping you'd left before my display.'

'Nope. I enjoyed every minute of it,' she said, teasing him. 'Must be all that swimming you do that keeps you fit and strong.'

He stopped dancing but held her close. 'Come swimming with me tomorrow morning,' he said, sounding impulsive.

'I'm not in your league when it comes to swimming. I haven't been swimming in the sea since I was a little girl.'

'Then it's time you did. The waters here are wonderful. And you'll be safe with me.'

She found herself agreeing before she realised the practicality of swimming with him. For a start, she didn't have a swimsuit; all she had was a bikini she'd thrown into her luggage when packing. It had been tossed in along with a selection of undies. The white bikini was fine for sunbathing in a London park, but swimming in the Cornish sea was something else. But then she looked up at Jake, and he was smiling at her, and she thought — what the heck. She'd wear it and damn the consequences.

'I'll pick you up at daylight. The sea is at its height then. You'll love it.'

'I can see Daisy's missing Roman Penhaligan,' Sharky said to Karen.

'Just as long as you're not missing the macaroon girl from Devon.'

'Give me a kiss to make sure,' Sharky said, teasingly, not expecting her to grab hold of him and kiss him passionately until he almost buckled.

Mrs Lemon and Woolley danced past them.

'It's lucky that Roman Penhaligan only has this summer party once a year,' said Mrs Lemon. 'Everyone ends up smooching.'

Woolley dipped Mrs Lemon in a tango move, the strength of his wiry old muscles taking her by surprise. He hadn't pinned her in a position like this in a long time. 'Nothing wrong with a bit of canoodling,' he said.

'Get away with you,' she said, flustered and flattered in equal measures. 'Silly old rascal.'

At the end of the night, the butler approached Daisy and offered to drive her back to the cottage, but she went back with Jake and Woolley. Jake had kept to soft drinks, wanting to keep his wits about him and in the hope that he could drive her home.

'Very well, Miss,' said the butler. 'Mr Penhaligan wanted me to give you this.' He handed her an envelope containing a cheque for payment for the painting. Daisy handed it back. 'It was a gift for Roman.'

The butler was taken aback, as if used to most women taking rather than giving anything of value to his employer. 'It's been a pleasure meeting you, Miss.'

'And you . . . I'm sorry, I don't know your name,' she said.

'Butler.'

'Yes, but —'

'George Butler,' he said. 'A very handy name or terribly confusing.'

Daisy giggled. 'Well, thank you Mr Butler.'

Jake drove the three of them home, stopping the car outside Franklin's cottage. It was a short drive from the castle, and Woolley had filled the conversation with raucous laughter and gossip from the events of the party.

Jake opened the car door and helped her out. He hesitated, on the brink of kissing her, when a flash of lightning ripped across the night sky. It reflected off the sea and a rain storm threatened.

Daisy stepped back from him and gazed up at the sky. 'Goodnight,' she said, and picked up the hem of her dress and ran into the cottage before the rain poured down.

Jake watched her go and then drove up the hill to his house.

Chapter Nine

Champagne and false promises

Sharky whistled happily as he stocked the shelf with bread and rolls in the health food shop next morning. Woolley stacked the shelves near the back of the shop.

Karen served Mrs Lemon who had come in to buy herb tea to flush the sweet sherry from her system.

'I don't know what went on with you and Sharky last night,' Mrs Lemon whispered to Karen, 'but you've obviously fluffed his feathers for him.'

'I didn't do anything you wouldn't do with Woolley Wolfe, mother.'

'Ssh!' said Mrs Lemon. 'Keep your voice down. The old goat's fancying his chances with me again.' Her cardigan was buttoned tight. 'I'm keeping my assets out of view until he cools down.'

Karen laughed.

'And remember, all hell's going to break loose soon with your meddling,' Mrs Lemon reminded her. 'Sebastian's on his way here.'

Karen sighed. 'I'm sorry I phoned him, but Sebastian wants Daisy back. He's ditched Celeste.'

Woolley was eavesdropping on their conversation. He stopped stacking the shelves and casually left the shop. Once outside the shop, he hurried straight to the coast where Jake and Daisy were swimming in the warm, turquoise sea.

He heard them laughing and enjoying themselves. Jake had lifted Daisy up and was about to splash her into the waves when Woolley shouted to them.

'Sebastian's coming to Cornwall.'

Jake and Daisy's world broke in two. Daisy swam to the shore to hear what had happened. Jake's steps felt heavy in the sand as he heard what Woolley had to say.

'Karen phoned him and blabbed that Daisy was hiding out in Franklin's cottage,' said Woolley.

Jake shook his head. The water fell from his dark hair and ran in rivulets down his hardened face. The muscles on his lean torso

85

tightened. His eyes, as blue as the sea, looked straight at Daisy. He could tell from her expression that everything was about to change.

Later in the day, Jake worked in his study while Daisy sat outside in the garden painting flower illustrations. The atmosphere had been tense between them, and both sought refuge in their respective work, until Jake's pent up anger boiled over.

Jake threw down his pen and marched out to the garden to confront her.

'I can't fathom why you'd want to meet up with Sebastian,' he said.

'He wants to talk to me. He phoned me at the cottage. We've agreed to have dinner in town tonight.'

Jake shook his head in disgust.

Her defences rose immediately. 'Woolley says I should meet with Sebastian and finish the relationship once and for all.'

'Sebastian is a manipulative rat. He'll lure you back to London with his lies.'

'I won't let him do that to me.'

'You're no match for Sebastian,' Jake said.

He turned and walked away down the hill.

Daisy sat in the garden and went over the things she wanted to say to Sebastian when she had dinner with him that night. Woolley's advice seemed reasonable. She should tell Sebastian exactly what she thought of his treacherous behaviour and ask him why he'd cheated on her for a year with Celeste. A year! That dagger dug deep.

She'd tell him straight, get it all out. Things needed to be said. Then they'd be finished.

She was still planning her defence, when she saw Woolley walking up the hill.

'Jake's not here,' she said. 'I think he's probably at the shop.'

'Yes, I saw the steam coming out his ears and body swerved him to come and talk to you.' He sat down on a garden chair and sighed heavily. 'Sebastian's here. He's checked into a hotel in the town.'

Daisy's knuckles turned white with the grip she had on her paintbrush. 'Is he coming up to the house do you think?'

'No, he's a wily one. He'll be sprucing himself up to have dinner with you. Remember, Sebastian's here for one reason — to entice you to go back with him to London.'

'Jake's not happy about any of this.'

'That's because he knows the lengths a man will go to when he wants something.'

'You certainly went for it last night with Mrs Lemon.'

'Yes, well, that was the drink,' said Woolley. 'She'd had too many sweet sherries.'

Daisy laughed.

'So keep a clear head tonight. Don't let Sebastian ply you with champagne and false promises.'

Sebastian had arranged a romantic candle–lit dinner with Daisy in the restaurant of a small hotel in the Cornish town where he was staying.

He looked as devilishly handsome as ever.

'Can you ever forgive me, Daisy? I made a mistake, a stupid mistake. The engagement was a whim. It made me realise that Celeste's not the one for me. I've been a complete idiot. Please give me another chance. I'm a wreck without you.'

Daisy sat in a state of upset and shock listening to Sebastian.

Woolley and Sharky were in the baker's van across the street watching them through the window of the restaurant. Sharky had Mrs Lemon's binoculars focussed on them.

Woolley peered at Daisy and Sebastian. 'What's Sebastian saying to her?' he said to Sharky.

'Lucky for us I can lip read at a hundred paces,' said Sharky, and then imitated Sebastian. 'Forgive me, Daisy. I love you.'

'Weasel,' said Woolley, pouring them each a cup of tea from a flask.

'There's iced fancies in the glove compartment.'

'Cheers,' said Woolley.

Sharky refocused the binoculars. 'Wait a minute. Sebastian's explaining why he called off the engagement with Celeste. He says that once she had the ring on her finger she became a monster, telling him what to do.'

'She was always hoity–toity,' said Woolley.

'Sebastian says Celeste's gone off on holiday, paid for by Franklin of course, to look for the artist who painted her portrait — apparently some mysterious fellow from Europe.'

'What's Daisy's reaction?'

Sharky sounded worried. 'He's getting to her. She's weakening.'

'Right. We've got some scheming to do.'

Back at Franklin's cottage that night, Daisy threw herself on the bed and beat her fists into the pillows. She wiped away the tears. Why did Sebastian have to come back now, just when she thought she was getting over him? Damn him! Damn him!

He'd told her to consider his offer of getting back together with him . . . to sleep on things. She knew she wouldn't sleep at all tonight. Jake had been right. She was no match for Sebastian. She'd had no intention of going back with him to London, and yet he'd had an answer for everything, and he'd made her feel guilty for not giving him a second chance. She'd avoided the champagne, but he'd plied her with plenty of promises, false or not, including the offer of moving into his house in London, making a fresh start, and the cherry on the cake — he'd asked her to marry him!

Jake knocked on her front door the next day. Daisy let him in. She'd obviously been crying.

Jake sounded angry. 'You let Sebastian upset you.'

'Don't you dare talk to me like that,' she said.

'Someone has to talk some sense into you.'

'Just because you've written books and concocted a cure for love doesn't mean you know anything about anything.'

'He got to you, didn't he?'

'If anyone got to, me, it's you, Jake.'

He shook his head.

She grabbed her portfolio of artwork and gave it to him. 'My work with you is finished. Here, find another artist.'

'If you'd taken the cure, Sebastian would've been history,' he said.

'Is that all you're bothered about — your precious remedy?'

'No of course not.'

'Yes it is. You've been trying to persuade me to take it since I arrived in Cornwall. So, okay, I'll do it!'

'You'll test the remedy?'

'Set it up for tonight.'

The muscles in his jaw tensed. 'Tonight. Seven o'clock.'

'Fine.'

Jake took the portfolio of artwork and stormed out, casting a parting shot over his shoulder. 'I'll add some paranoia for good measure.'

'Do that,' she shouted and slammed the door behind him.

Woolley and Jake argued in his study.

'You can't let her take it,' said Woolley.

'It was her idea,' said Jake.

'Clearly she's not thinking straight.'

'A dose of the remedy will straighten her brain.'

'You risk losing her love. She doesn't love Sebastian.'

'You could've fooled me.'

'You're only fooling yourself, Jake.'

Jake started to prepare the study for the test. He got his charts out and some of the bottles of herbal essence.

'We're going ahead with it tonight. Witnesses are needed to validate the test. Everyone is welcome to come along,' said Jake. 'And if you see Mr Greenie, tell him to bring his video camera. If it's anything like the fiasco he filmed at the party it'll be well worth seeing.'

The townspeople were holding their breath. By now, everyone who was close to Daisy and Jake knew deep down they were falling in love.

Woolley, Sharky, Mrs Lemon and Karen spoke in a huddle in the main street.

'If Daisy takes the cure, it won't be Sebastian it'll cure her of — it'll be Jake,' said Woolley. 'I know it's a cure for lovesickness, but I think Daisy's over Sebastian, and now with all the upset and arguing today with Jake, it could change how she feels about him.'

Mrs Lemon folded her arms tightly across her cardigan. 'We can't let that happen.'

Karen shrugged. 'Jake's never fancied me anyway.'

'He must be mad,' said Sharky.

Karen smiled.

On the other side of the street, Mrs Lemon saw Sebastian. 'You'd better be at Jake Wolfe's house tonight at seven o'clock, Sebastian. You're the cause of all this trouble.'

Sebastian looked perplexed. He walked away.

'Remember the plan for tonight,' Woolley said to them. 'I'm betting Daisy won't take the cure. I think she'll bottle out at the last minute. But if she doesn't, everyone knows what to do . . .'

Karen nodded. 'I cause a distraction.'

Sharky spoke up. 'While Woolley and I grab the remedy from Daisy so she doesn't get a chance to take it.'

'What about Roman Penhaligan?' said Karen.

'He's not going. He's back with Daphne in London,' said Woolley. 'It's up to us to make sure the plan works.'

It was almost seven o'clock. Daisy was dressed and ready to go to Jake's house when there was a knock on the door.

Daisy brightened up, thinking it was Jake. She hurried to open the door.

'Jake?' she said, before realising it wasn't him. She sounded downcast. 'Sebastian.'

'Everyone's talking about you,' said Sebastian. 'You really don't believe Jake Wolfe has created some nonsense cure for love?'

'I don't know what to think, but the remedy is harmless, so I'm going to drink it and see if it works.'

'If it does, you wouldn't love me any more.'

'But you think it's nonsense,' she argued.

Sebastian didn't sound quite so confident. 'Jake's full of surprises.'

'So am I,' said Daisy.

Chapter Ten

Would you take it?

Everyone was gathered in Jake's study waiting for Daisy to arrive. Grey storm clouds brought an early twilight to the evening, and from the front window of the study the sea shimmered like silver.

The study was warmly lit with table lamps and wall lights. The cure for love remedy was set up on Jake's desk. Two desk lamps lit up the bottles, jars and glass phials of coloured liquids. Various charts and reference books were lying on the desk. Jake was reading from the notes.

Mr Greenie had the video camera set up and filmed everything that Jake was doing.

Sharky stood next to Karen and held her hand. She made no attempt to pull it away.

'Sharky and Karen are getting on well,' Woolley whispered Mrs Lemon. 'He must have tempted her with a custard flan.'

She nodded. 'It's been a long time coming. He's always liked her. Despite the silly things we tease him about, he's got a decent nature. Karen could do a lot worse than marry him.'

'Marry him? You think he'll marry her?' said Woolley.

'I saw a wedding ring in her tea cup, and a big fancy cake,' Mrs Lemon confided.

The cuckoo clock creaked and spluttered that it was seven o'clock as Daisy and Sebastian arrived. Sebastian could've sworn the cuckoo gave him a steely–eyed glare before juddering back inside the clock.

Jake had the sleeves of his white shirt rolled up and was busy mixing the remedy, carefully adding the ingredients from the bottles. He glanced at Daisy and Sebastian as they walked into the study. It was torture for him to see them together. Daisy looked beautiful in her little silver dress. Sebastian wore a lightweight grey suit and an arrogant grin.

Sebastian acknowledged Jake with a curt nod. 'Jake.'

Jake returned the gesture. 'Sebastian.' Then he muttered to himself. 'Swine.'

Daisy looked at Jake, but he busied himself with the remedy. She'd been hoping he'd talk her out of taking it, though from the determined expression on his face there was no chance of that. Sebastian had driven her up to Jake's house, still trying to talk her out of taking the cure for love. He'd been the one who had broken her heart, and now here he was in a room full of people who despised him, defying them and trying to win her back. She couldn't help but admire him for that.

'Remember the plan,' Woolley whispered to Sharky.

Sharky gave him a knowing wink. So did Mrs Lemon and Karen.

'Every time I come down to this town I get caught up in their madness,' Sebastian said to Daisy.

'Then you should've stayed in London,' said Daisy.

'What's in the remedy?' Karen said to Jake.

Jake explained while mixing. 'Lots of herbs and essences, mixed to match Daisy's strongest emotions. And various other ingredients that frankly I'm too agitated to divulge.'

'Don't forget a few drops of paranoia,' said Daisy.

'A dash of spite wouldn't go amiss either.' Jake added a dash of the essence from a bottle labelled SPITE.

Sebastian was aghast. 'You're not really going to drink that are you?' he said to Daisy.

Jake cut in. 'That's what she's here for.'

'You don't have to do this,' Sebastian said to Daisy. 'We can leave now and go home to London. We can make a fresh start.'

Daisy looked at Sebastian. For a moment she hesitated.

'Come home with me, Daisy. You don't belong with these strangers,' said Sebastian.

'I know more about these strangers in one week of being here than I know about my supposed friends in London. There are no secrets down here. Just blunt but honest truths.'

Sharky smiled.

'Almost ready,' Jake announced.

Woolley shook his head. 'You're both making a terrible mistake,' he said to Jake and Daisy. 'It's not too late to change your minds.'

'Someone else will come along and you can test the remedy on them,' Sharky said to Jake.

'Broken hearts are ten a penny,' said Mrs Lemon.

Jake poured the mixture into a glass phial. It looked like turquoise blue water.

'Don't do it, Daisy,' Woolley warned her.

Jake handed the phial to Daisy. 'You can back out if you want to.'

Daisy held the phial. She hesitated. Her thoughts rewound to some of the things that had happened recently. . .

She pictured Sebastian in the London park telling her he was going to Italy. And how he'd said when she asked if there was anything else she could do for him, 'Yes, love me forever.'

She remembered Sebastian and Celeste celebrating their engagement at Franklin's company, and then torching his love letters in the toaster before driving off to Cornwall.

She recalled the first time she'd met Jake Wolfe in his shop and how everyone knew all about her business.

And the day she'd had a green nose and Jake had said, 'If you hate Sebastian, why don't you let me help you? If I were you, I'd take anything less than poison to get him out of my system.'

And the night Jake pinned her to the lawn when she'd attacked him with a stuffed haddock, and felt that first spark of romance from him. Then as Mr Greenie fixed the fuses by candlelight, Jake had said, 'If a woman like you was in love with me, I'd never dream of betraying her.'

And Jake's warning to her. 'Sebastian is a manipulative rat. He'll lure you back to London with his lies.'

'I won't let him do that to me,' she'd said.

'You're no match for Sebastian,' Jake said.

She thought about the candle–lit dinner in Cornwall with Sebastian where he'd said, 'Please give me another chance. I'm a wreck without you.'

She still felt the sting of Jake's words. 'He got to you, didn't he?'

Jake was right. And tonight Sebastian had tried to persuade her to leave with him. 'You don't have to do this. We can leave now and go home to London. We can make a fresh start.'

The flashbacks ended as she blinked back to the present. She held the phial of blue liquid and looked at Jake and then at Sebastian.

Everyone held their breath.

For a moment it seemed as if she wasn't going to drink it, then she surprised them all.

93

Everything felt as if it was happening in slow motion. Daisy lifted the liquid to her lips.

'No,' Woolley shouted.

At the last minute Jake realised the mistake he was making and tried to stop her.

Woolley, Sharky, Mrs Lemon and Karen all tried to stop her. Karen didn't have time to cause a distraction. Their plan didn't work.

Daisy outmanoeuvred them all and, to their horror, drank the remedy.

They were shocked into silence.

Jake approached her. 'Daisy?'

Daisy didn't respond. She seemed slightly dazed.

'When does the remedy take effect?' Woolley said to Jake.

'As soon as it hits the system — it's like drinking a measure of whisky.'

Everyone stared at Daisy.

'Has it worked? How do you feel?' Sebastian said to her.

'I feel…better…not entirely okay, but it's taken the edge off some things.'

'What things?' said Jake.

Daisy looked at Sebastian. 'I can look at Sebastian and not want to rip his heart out through his eye–balls when I think of him with Celeste.'

Jake was delighted. Sebastian was uncertain.

Daisy looked at Karen. 'And I'm not as mad at Karen for phoning Sebastian.'

Woolley sounded anxious. 'What about Jake? How do you feel about him?'

She looked at Jake. 'The same.'

'What do you mean the same?' said Jake.

'The same as I did before I drank the remedy,' said Daisy.

'Be more specific,' said Sebastian.

Daisy sighed. 'I've learned something since I came to Cornwall. I've learned how to be blunt but honest. So, specifically, I don't love you, Sebastian. I despise you. You are everything I hate in a man.' She paused and looked at Jake. 'I'm falling in love with Jake.'

Jake's heart leaped at this news and he smiled at Daisy.

Sebastian was distraught. There was a small amount of the remedy in the phial. Sebastian made a grab for it. Mrs Lemon beat him to it.

'Oh no you don't, Sebastian. You're in love with yourself more than with Daisy.' Mrs Lemon handed the phial to Jake.

'I'm going back home to London, away from the madness and mayhem of Cornwall,' Sebastian said to Daisy.

'No one hurry to stop him,' said Sharky.

Sebastian left and slammed the door.

Daisy looked at Jake and then her expression changed. She hurried after Sebastian.

She opened the front door and called to him. 'Sebastian.'

Sebastian paused and turned around, feeling hopeful. 'Yes, Daisy?'

Daisy edged her words with venom. 'Don't come fucking back!'

There was a loud cheer from the others in the house.

Jake looked at the remedy phial. 'Too many drops of spite,' he muttered to himself.

Daisy went back into the study.

'I'll make us all a nice cup of tea,' said Mrs Lemon.

Jake pulled Daisy aside. 'How do you feel now?'

'A lot better,' she said, seeing Sebastian drive off.

Jake whispered to Woolley. 'We'll need to be careful until we find out if the remedy has any side effects — nothing horrible, but I may have been a bit heavy handed with the spite.'

'Why didn't the cure for love work on her?' said Woolley.

'Because she's not broken–hearted any more. She doesn't love Sebastian.'

Woolley nodded and then spoke to Daisy. 'I think you should stay down here for a little while longer until you feel up to going back to London.'

'Franklin phoned me today. He says he's happy for me to email my illustrations to him, and we'll work out the future from there,' said Daisy.

Mrs Lemon brought in a tray of tea and biscuits and was arguing with Karen. 'I can't believe you were going to run after Sebastian and throw yourself at him. Look what happened the last time.'

'I wasn't going to throw myself at him,' said Karen.

'Everyone was staring at the two of you from the bric–a–brac stall,' Sharky reminded her teasingly.

'My earring got caught on his fly fishing tackle —'

'Yeah, right,' said Sharky.

Woolley laughed.

'And what are you laughing at?' said Karen. 'I know all about you and my mother!'

'Right,' said Mrs Lemon. 'That's enough tittle–tattle. Who wants a crumbly biscuit?'

Jake was astounded and glared at Woolley. 'You humped Mrs Lemon?'

Sharky nearly choked on his biscuit. 'Still life in the old dog yet, eh? You too, Woolley.'

They all start squabbling.

Daisy muttered to herself. 'Yes, a quiet break in the country should do me the world of good...'

Over the next few weeks, Daisy finished the illustrations for Jake's book, but there was one flower missing. He planned to set out soon to look for the elusive blue flower that was a key ingredient in his cure for love. He would dive for it off the coast of Cornwall. Then, after testing the latest version of the remedy, his book would be ready for publication.

Jake thought that Daisy should go with him. He was going to need an illustrator, especially one he was crazy about.

They set out in Woolley's boat on a hot summer's day. The wind caught the white sails, and the sea was a beautiful turquoise blue.

'I know I've made mistakes, Daisy, but I'll never risk losing you again,' said Jake. He wrapped her in his arms and kissed her passionately. 'I love you, Daisy,' he said, before diving into the sea.

Would he find the flower he was searching for? Yes, she thought he would. She'd brought her sketch pad and paints so she could capture it as perfectly as he'd described it to her.

She relaxed on the deck of the boat. Now that she was living in Cornwall there was plenty of romance in the air. Sharky was planning to propose to Karen, and everyone knew she would say yes. They also envisaged that the engagement cake would be a whopper. As for Mrs Lemon's relationship with Woolley, she'd unbuttoned her cardigan recently so that was a start. And by all accounts, Roman Penhaligan was still living it up in London with Daphne.

Daisy breathed in the fresh sea air and thought back to how her life had been. All the upset with Sebastian had faded; it was part of the past. Sebastian may have broken her heart, but Jake turned out to be her true cure for love.

End

About the Author:

Follow De-ann on Instagram @deann.black

De-ann Black is a bestselling author, scriptwriter and former newspaper journalist. She has over 80 books published. Romance, crime thrillers, espionage novels, action adventure. And children's books (non-fiction rocket science books and children's fiction). She became an Amazon All-Star author in 2014 and 2015.

She previously worked as a full-time newspaper journalist for several years. She had her own weekly columns in the press. This included being a motoring correspondent where she got to test drive cars every week for the press for three years.

Before being asked to work for the press, De-ann worked in magazine editorial writing everything from fashion features to social news. She was the marketing editor of a glossy magazine. She is also a professional artist and illustrator. Fabric design, dressmaking, sewing, knitting and fashion are part of her work.

Additionally, De-ann has always been interested in fitness, and was a fitness and bodybuilding champion, 100 metre runner and mountaineer. As a former N.A.B.B.A. Miss Scotland, she had a weekly fitness show on the radio that ran for over three years.

De-ann trained in Shukokai karate, boxing, kickboxing, Dayan Qigong and Jiu Jitsu. She is currently based in Scotland.

Her colouring books and embroidery design books are available in paperback. These include Floral Nature Embroidery Designs and Scottish Garden Embroidery Designs.

Find out more at: www.de-annblack.com

Printed in Great Britain
by Amazon

84122946R00061